The Gardens of Byzantium

The Gardens of Byzantium

J. F. Hughes

The Gardens of Byzantium
All Rights Reserved

ISBN 979-8-218-21981-9
Cover Design by Erin Hughes
Maps by Amber Leach and Mallory Lee

To my lovely and loving Kaitlin,
Who is the star of the greatest love story I know,
Where each chapter is better than the last,
And the story never ends…

MUSICAL ACCOMPANIMENT

For your enjoyment, the author has curated a chapter-by-chapter musical accompaniment for this novel. You may choose to find your favorite versions of these classical compositions, or you may utilize the playlist provided at www.JFHbooks.com.

CHAPTER I
Sonata quasi una Fantasia, Piano Sonata No. 14 in C-Sharp Minor, Op. 27 No. 2, I. Adagio Sostenuto
Ludwig Van Beethoven

CHAPTER II
Capricho Árabe
Francisco Tárrega

CHAPTER III
Trio Sonata in D minor, Op. 1 No. 12, "La Follia" RV 63
Antonio Vivaldi

CHAPTER IV
Mallorca, Op. 202
Isaac Albéniz

CHAPTER V
Violin Concerto No. 4 in D Minor, MS. 60 - III. Rondo galante. Andantino gaio
Niccolò Paganini

"For there is a single harmony.
Just as the world forms a single
body comprising all bodies,
so fate forms a single purpose,
comprising all purposes."

-Marcus Aurelius

Prologue

We stand at the crossroads of West and East, on our peninsula that bridges Europe and Asia. This is the crown jewel of the Roman Empire: Constantinople. When our Emperor Constantine chose Byzantium, it was nothing but a small Greek harbor town. Now, our reinvigorated city has grown to become one of the largest and most prosperous in all of God's earthly domain.

And while our Western cousins in Rome were overcome by a tide of woe, God, in his infinite mercy, chose to spare us. When the barbarians set their sights on our walls and gates, he chose to spare us. When we ignored his example of mercy and burned our own city, killing our brothers, he chose to spare us. And when the plague arrived on our shores and reaped its sorrowful harvest, still he chose to spare us. Mercy beyond what we lowly sinners deserved, all because our unshakeable faith in the Father, Son, and Holy Spirit remained firm.

And now, the Persians, who worship the flame and have chosen to remain ignorant of God's teaching and salvation, seek to take this city from us. They have tried for twenty years now to bring death to us, God's faithful servants. And again, God will spare us. Indeed, more than sparing us, he has brought to us an Emperor who will lead us to victory. Hail Emperor Heraclius!

So, my brothers and sisters, we have nothing to fear. God's mercy is limitless, but we are often too blinded by our sinfulness to see it. It is because of the sinfulness of man that his mercy is most transformative, most sublime, when it is bestowed by one sinner on another. But we are faced with an army of heathens who would not even receive mercy were it offered and most certainly will not give mercy were it asked.

Thus you shall march with God's servant Heraclius at your head, off to battle. And God will reward your faith, and God will save the Romans!

The Patriarch Sergius,
To the assembled army in Constantinople,
Easter Morning, 622 A.D.

THE
NEAR
EAST
622 A.D.

CONSTANTINOPLE
(BYZANTIUM)

TARSUS

EDESSA

ANTIOCH

LAODICEA

GABALA

PALMYRA

BERYTUS

CTESIPHON

DAMASCUS

TYRE

ALEXANDRIA

Chapter I
The Prison at Antioch
(622 A.D.)

"Perhaps three months," Antonius said to the cold, silent ground.

But how could he be sure? He had every intention of counting the days, but now even his thoughts exhausted what little strength he had. He often thought the cruelest part was not the hunger, the pain, or the darkness, but that he was denied the honor of dying in battle. For months he had fought alongside Emperor Heraclius as he marched his army through Bithynia,

Galatia, Cappadocia… and to the very threshold of the holy lands in Syria and Judaea. Victories came naturally, and the blood of many Persians stained the haft of Antonius' spear.

Then one day, Antonius and half a dozen others volunteered to trek to the outskirts of Tarsus under cover of darkness to assess the strength of the Persian garrison there. He and his men reached the foothills north of Tarsus and could see a glow in the distance. The warm light of the city and the horizon beyond where stars met the inky darkness of the *Mare Nostrum* would be the last thing Antonius would see as a free man. The snapping of a twig and the shout of one of his men were the last things he remembered.

He awoke from his daze periodically over the next few days, confused and with splitting pains in his head. When he finally gathered his senses, he had only cold, cavernous walls to look upon. Antonius gazed upwards and saw the extent of his predicament—the rough walls of the enclosure ended far above the floor of the pit. Beyond that, he could only make out dim light and the sandstone blocks of whatever structure he was under. He sat for a long time, not thinking of anything other than his hunger and thirst.

Eventually, he could not say how much time had passed, a silhouette appeared over the rim of the pit. The silhouette bellowed a sharp, echoing shout and proceeded to lower a bucket into the pit with a rope. Antonius scrambled toward the bucket, finding his muscles weaker than he had expected. Inside the bucket were a carafe of water and some stale pieces of bread, which Antonius greedily devoured, saving nothing but a few crumbs. The very presence of food in his stomach provoked a wave of nausea, but his hunger soon returned.

Unfortunately, his jailor's silhouette was not as quick to return. When the jailor did return, he lowered the same bucket with the same meager rations. Antonius guessed that these

2

meals were to come but once a day. He cursed his fate, and after the seventh day, the sharpest agony was no longer the hunger gnawing at his gut. Instead, *not knowing what came next* began gnawing at his mind.

The next time the silhouette appeared over the edge of the pit, Antonius shouted, "Persian swine! Lower yourself in the bucket, and I will eat your liver instead!" The jailor simply spat into the pit and left without leaving bread or water for the thinning prisoner. Antonius shouted with all the strength he could conjure, "Coward!"

Another full day passed before he ate again. More water and stale bread. Hunger was now a constant companion, made worse by the lack of other occurrences. But that very evening, the monotony was broken when three silhouettes appeared over the rim of the pit. One of the figures held out a lantern, casting dancing shadows onto the sandstone walls high above Antonius' head. Illuminated in the lantern light was the sharp nose of the man standing between the others. The amber light glinted off his breastplate, bracers, and buckle. The man reached out to his left, grabbing something from the figure beside him and tossing it down into the pit. Another scrap of bread for Antonius, reduced to the stature of a dog.

The man stood at the rim of the pit for a moment, staring down at Antonius, who was staring right back, able only to see his captor's nose and armor.

The man sighed heavily and then spoke, "I know you must have many questions. I am Ardashir, the *argbadh* of this fortress. You are one of Emperor Heraclius' scouts, but not a very good one, it seems. My men captured you quite readily, just north of Tarsus, and now you are my guests here in Antioch."

Guests? Antonius straightened up and spoke out, "The others are alive?"

"Only two of your men survived the journey here, although they may wish they hadn't, depending on how you choose to move forward."

Antonius spoke slowly in a weakened, gravelly voice, "What does that mean?"

"It means you give me the information I need, and I let your brethren go free. They have already informed me that you were the ranking officer amongst them… it is true, is it not?"

Antonius knew that none of his men would reveal this information. It could not be extracted from them, no matter what method the Persians used. Antonius' men were strong. Loyal. Nevertheless, he was indeed the ranking officer, and he decided that letting this be known might spare his comrades some suffering.

"Yes, it is true. I am Antonius Andronicus, *pentarch* of the vanguard, in service to Emperor Heraclius, whom you will certainly have the pleasure of meeting."

Ardashir laughed heartily, his teeth glinting in the lantern light as he did so.

He spoke again in nearly perfect Greek, "That would be most wonderful! I have heard so much about this Emperor Heraclius and his poorly trained vanguards. I look forward to the day when I can teach him to fight like a real warrior. If he shows enough respect, I may even allow him to keep his life and serve as a eunuch in my court."

Now it was Antonius' turn to laugh. "Emperor Heraclius has marched at his leisure through all of Anatolia, only slowing down to mock your Persian *warriors* who were too busy soiling themselves to mount a defense!"

Ardashir laughed again, as did his men, and Antonius followed suit.

"You are witty, *pentarch,* but time will reveal all. For the moment, I advise you to consider your circumstances. Your men will benefit greatly from your cooperation. I will return tomorrow." Ardashir and his two guards turned to leave.

"How do I know my men are still alive?" Antonius shouted after them.

Ardashir's voice echoed down the pit. "They tell me their names are Urbicus and Francio."

The sound of their footsteps receded in tandem with the glow of the lantern light. Antonius listened intently for a long while, trying to discern anything about the space above him, but his efforts were futile. He was restless and found no sleep. His mind was wrestling with the idea that Urbicus and Francio might already be dead. They might have simply told Ardashir their names before he killed them. Antonius had no way of knowing. He was reminded again that *not knowing* was a worse enemy than hunger or thirst.

* * *

The following day, Ardashir returned, flanked this time by four silhouettes. The silhouette to his left cast a thick braided rope down into the pit. Near its end, the rope divided into four strands, each of which ended at the corners of a net.

"I hope you are well rested, *pentarch*. There is much we have to discuss today. Please have a seat. I have a piece of lamb and a cup of wine ready for you."

Antonius obliged, if only for the break in the monotony. He sat, and Ardashir's guards pulled the rope taut, enclosing Antonius in the net. His thinned muscles provided no cushion against the ropes, which seemed to eat into his very bones. As he was hauled over the edge of the pit, he noticed the air was slightly warmer. He could see little. His weakened eyes were blinded by the light from the men's torches. Ardashir's men carried Antonius in the net, then down a hallway into a room that was empty save for a cask and a wooden post. The guards shackled one of Antonius' ankles in iron, chained him to the post, and released him from the net.

It took more effort than Antonius expected to stand up, and by the time he did, a servant was placing a plate and cup on the upright cask. The scent of freshly cooked meat hit Antonius' nose, and he salivated immediately. He fought to prevent himself from leaping toward the cask and devouring the meal. He didn't want to give the Persians the satisfaction of seeing how desperately hungry he was.

Ardashir motioned to the cask, saying, "Please eat. I told you lamb and wine, and I am a man of my word."

Antonius said nothing to Ardashir. And after a pause that was long enough to satisfy Antonius' pride, he stepped over to the cask and bit into the lamb leg on the plate. Antonius felt a rush—an ecstatic relief that is only experienced by those unfortunate enough to have known true hunger and fortunate enough to have found food again. He ate greedily and paused only to drink from the cup. It was half full of a watered wine, which was no less satisfying than the meat. The feast was over as soon as it began, and the servant retrieved the plate and cup.

"So," Ardashir began. "I suppose you have presumed that my hospitality today is not simply for hospitality's sake." Antonius again said nothing, instead studying the features of Ardashir's face, his sharp nose and jaw, his worn leather skin and dark eyes. "What I need from you, *pentarch*, is for you to share with me your knowledge of Heraclius and his army. Now, I am sure you have guessed that the Emperor's assault on Tarsus was easily defeated. Perhaps this was due to the capture of his vanguard?" At this, Ardashir motioned to Antonius and smiled, and Antonius could see the guards grinning smugly. "No matter," the Persian continued, "I am interested in the man himself. I am of the belief that it is only right for a man to know his adversary."

6

There was a long silence before Antonius spoke, "Emperor Heraclius is a great warrior. The kind of warrior who inspires an unshakeable loyalty in the men under his command. The kind of loyalty that remains even if they are captured."

"Is that so?" Ardashir replied while nodding in feigned admiration. "Well, I must admit, Emperor Heraclius would be pleased to know that neither of his soldiers would tell me anything of his plans, no matter how much I tried to persuade them. Although, it occurred to me after several conversations with the brave soldiers that they might not be as familiar with Emperor Heraclius' ambitions as his valiant *pentarch*!"

"Where are they?" Antonius demanded.

"Not far. Not far at all. Perhaps you would like to say hello?" Ardashir motioned to the guard standing nearest the entrance to the room, who left immediately. After some time, Antonius heard the sounds of iron dragging on the sandstone floor in the hallways and the muffled barked commands of a Persian guard. The sound grew louder until a ghastly figure appeared at the entrance. It was a gaunt shell of a man, and through the bloodied bruises and chains, Antonius was able to recognize a familiar face.

"Urbicus!"

To Antonius' horror, Urbicus could not even muster the strength to answer and was quickly dragged back down the hallway from which he came. Just a moment later, the horror repeated itself as another battered man was pushed to the floor at the entranceway.

"Francio…" Antonius said despairingly.

Francio looked up from the ground where he had been thrown and managed to say, "We gave nothing!" before he was dragged out of view by his arms.

"It is true, you see," Ardashir began. "Neither of them has spoken a word beyond pleasantries. And it is not for want of trying! Narseh, my lieutenant, exhausted himself, beating the two as if they were donkeys. And like donkeys, they would not say a word!"

At this, Antonius felt his rage well up from deep within. He lunged at Ardashir, only to be held back by the iron cutting into his ankle. The guards pounced, beat, and kicked Antonius, then ensnared him in the net he had arrived in. He had no more strength to resist. All his anger was in vain.

As he was dragged out of the room, Ardashir called after him, "You would do well to consider your circumstances, *pentarch...*"

* * *

Antonius awoke to a howling agony in his head and body. He lay sprawled on the bottom of the cruelly familiar pit that was now his home. The pain kept his mind occupied for hours, but as soon as he reached a position on his back that allowed some minor relief, a slew of other miseries came to the fore. Thirst... hunger... anger... frustration... despair... all the hellish things a man can experience at once, made worse by the knowledge that nothing could be done about it.

After some time, he heard approaching footsteps. Soon the silhouette of the jailor appeared at the edge of the pit, lowering a bucket of stale bread and water to Antonius. Antonius ate, but even chewing had become exhausting for his bruised and famished body. For many weeks, the once-daily meal was the only break in the dark silence down in that hole. But then, at the moment of Antonius' greatest despair, a curious thing happened.

A noise. Footsteps echoing gently off the rock walls of the pit. There was something different. These were not the heavy, brutal footsteps of a soldier or guard. These sounded gentle and cautious, like the footsteps of a mouse or a thief.

The footsteps approached the edge of the pit, and a shadow was cast, not of a mouse or a thief, but of a girl. The girl peered into the pit for a moment and then retreated, leaving Antonius puzzled. Before he could come up with an explanation, the girl's shadow reappeared, this time lowering the bucket and rope.

Antonius watched in silence as the bucket made its slow descent, and when it arrived, he peered in, seeing bread, a few dates, and a few grapes. Antonius' heart leapt. He wasted no time, and the first taste of fresh bread and fruit rang through him like a bell. The girl clumsily began hauling the emptied bucket back up and out of the pit, and her silhouette pitter-pattered out of sight just as suddenly as it had arrived. After the euphoria of the unexpected feast subsided, Antonius sat wondering. He did not know what to make of this strange visit.

The following day, the jailor arrived on schedule, delivering the regular meal of stale bread and water. And then, a few hours later, the same mouse-like steps echoed off the walls. Again the girl lowered the bucket to Antonius. This time, there was a small piece of lamb, some cheese, and more grapes. He devoured the lamb. He would eat the rest in a few hours when the hunger returned. The girl pulled the bucket away and departed.

On the third day, the girl did not appear at all. It was a devastating disappointment for Antonius, who had nothing else to look forward to. He spent the entire day wondering only if she would return. To his great delight, the girl appeared again on the fourth day. The bucket was lowered, but inside were only a few pieces of bread. His hopes of lamb and honey were dashed, but he ate nonetheless.

Around the time he was expecting his jailor the following day, four guards appeared and lowered the rope net. Antonius debated the wisdom of allowing himself to be pulled from the pit again, but his thoughts were of Urbicus and Francio.

I must go.

He was pulled up and carried down the sandstone hall, his eyes struggling to see. He was brought to the same room and shackled to the same wooden post. Two of the guards left, and two remained, posting themselves at the entrance to the room. Ardashir was nowhere to be seen.

Eventually, a man entered the room and placed a leather satchel on the cask. He was tall and thin, with scars on his cheek, his neck, and his hand. He had dark, sunken eyes and moved with deliberate languidness.

When he spoke, his raspy voice did not go much beyond a whisper, "As you may have guessed, I am Narseh. Ardashir asked me to visit you because of my... well, because men tend to tell me things that they would not tell anyone else. I have several things I need from you, and if you provide them, I will provide you with food and drink and perhaps a more amenable sleeping arrangement. If you do not answer forthrightly, I am afraid I will have to find a way to persuade you. Do you understand what I have said to you?"

Antonius looked Narseh in the eyes and said calmly, "Go to hell."

Narseh smiled. "A defiant start. Not unexpected, however."

He turned and barked a word in Persian to the guards, who turned and entered the room. They grabbed Antonius by the arms and placed his chest against the wooden post rising out of the floor. They proceeded to bind his wrists together and strap his waist to the post. Antonius was helpless to resist in his famished state. He could hear Narseh walk to the satchel on the cask and unroll it. A moment later, Antonius heard the sharp crack of a whip.

"Now... how many men-at-arms were with Emperor Heraclius when he reached Tarsus?"

Antonius spoke, "More men than there are grains of sand in Syria."

Immediately, the pain shot through Antonius' back as the crack of the whip rang in his ears. Barely a moment passed before the second lash came down on Antonius' shoulder.

Narseh said, "I am certain that Heraclius is a capable general, able to lead many men. But *surely* you cannot expect me to believe that, *pentarch*! Think! And I ask again, how many men-at-arms were with the Emperor at Tarsus?"

Antonius was still recovering from the strikes, the stings barely lessening in intensity.

Through his teeth, Antonius said, "I cannot say how many were at Tarsus."

Narseh scoffed, "Of course you know, *pentarch*! Don't take me for a fool."

Antonius replied with feigned earnestness, "I am speaking the truth. I seem to have suffered a small bump on the head at that time. My memory has not been the same since..."

The lashes rained down in rapid succession. Once, twice, three times. These lashes were more severe, and Antonius could feel blood trailing down his back.

"Insolence will not get you very far," Narseh explained. "You see, over the years I have gained a mastery of interrogations such as this. I have found that there are only two types of men—those who beg before the first lash and those who beg before the hundredth lash. Make no mistake, *pentarch*, your show of stubbornness and wit have no effect on me because I have seen men who are more stubborn than you beg for mercy, and I have seen men who were stronger than you beg for death." A chill ran through Antonius' bones. Narseh continued, "You will tell me what I need to know. It is

11

simply a matter of how tired I will be when you do. Now, *how many men were with Heraclius at Tarsus?*"

Antonius spoke quietly through his clenched teeth, "Go… to… hell."

The whip came down in a fury again. Half a dozen lashes this time, and Antonius fell to his knees, arms still wrapped around the post. He felt a pain that was beyond his experience. It was a pain that blocked out all else.

Narseh remained silent for some time before speaking again, "Have you broken already, *pentarch*? We have only just begun!"

* * *

Antonius lay face down at the bottom of the pit. He was one half-step from being a dead man. Ardashir's lieutenant had interrogated him for hours. Antonius had given him nothing, but he had paid a steep price. His back was bloodied, and he didn't even have the strength to sit upright. Between the blinding flashes of pain that occurred with each movement, Antonius confronted the situation. He would likely die either here, at the bottom of the pit, or bound to a whipping post at the hands of the enemy. There was a strange relief in the thought. Imprisoned and resigned to death, Antonius was liberated from the mundane concerns of ordinary men. The strangeness of the realization caught Antonius by surprise, and he laughed to himself. Quietly at first, but then louder, until a coughing fit ended the momentary escape.

He lost all sense of time. There was no rest, only hunger, pain, and despair. Antonius knew he was strong, but he was not sure how much more he could take before he broke. More hours passed in silence as he lay curled on the cold floor. Then, just as he was drifting toward sleep, he thought he heard a familiar noise. Was this his imagination? No, he heard it again! He attempted to sit upright and winced as his back reminded him of his wounds. The quiet footsteps of the unknown girl echoed down the walls to Antonius' ears. And sure enough, the familiar silhouette of the young woman appeared at the edge of the pit, lowering the bucket again. When the bucket reached him on the floor, he peered in and, to his delight, saw more lamb and bread.

Antonius began to devour his feast, but as he did so, he noticed one other item in the bucket: a glass vial. Inside the vial was a waxy, dark paste. Antonius brought the vial to his nose and inhaled. "Myrrh," he whispered to himself. The bucket was hauled up, and the girl left quietly. Antonius finished his lamb and saved his bread. He picked up the vial, opened it, and smeared some of the resin on his fingertips. Again, he inhaled the warm, radiant scent of the myrrh and something else he could not identify.

Even back in Byzantium, a salve of this quality would not be cheap. But in Antioch during a war, the price must be much higher. *Who is this girl?* Antonius wondered to himself. He gingerly pressed the salve on the areas of his back that he could reach. The initial sting gave way to numbness, much to his relief. Having now eaten and addressed his wounds as best he could, Antonius fell into a heavy sleep.

...He dreamt he was back in Byzantium at sunset, overlooking the waters of the Propontis and the Bosphorus. The sky to the west was a brilliant mosaic of orange, crimson, and purple. In the distance, to the east, he could see the masts of dozens of ships in the river. On their flags, he could see the Chi-Rho, *the insignia of God's army. Beyond them, he saw storm clouds rolling in, and soon some of the ships in the harbor were ablaze. The winds picked up, and the fiery glow soon danced on the city walls. He heard women and children*

*screaming and the pounding of a battering ram on the iron
gate over and over and over...*

He was startled awake by the bucket hitting the ground
next to his head. The jailor was delivering the daily crumbs.

* * *

For weeks, Antonius' life was a dismal cycle of near-
starvation and torture, followed by the merciful interventions
of the mysterious young woman. Only the young woman's
charity kept Antonius alive, both spiritually and physically. She
gave him hope, and without hope, there was nothing. But who
she was and why she chose to so faithfully deliver him succor
and nourishment remained a puzzle to Antonius.

Sergius, the Patriarch of Byzantium, had spoken to the
soldiers before they departed on their expedition into Anatolia.
The men stood in formation on the grounds of the Hippodrome,
with Emperor Heraclius at their head. Sergius had just presided
over Easter Mass and was blessing the gathered troops. He
spoke at length about the righteousness of their mission, the
survival of the empire, and the duty of all Romans to fight for
Christendom. But one thing the Patriarch said came back to
Antonius' mind as he lay nearly lifeless on the cold ground of
the pit.

*"God's mercy is limitless, but we are often too blinded
by our sinfulness to see it. But it is because of the sinfulness of
man that his mercy is most transformative, most sublime when
it is bestowed by one sinner on another..."*

Here Antonius was—hungry, beaten, and alone. Yet the
mercy of another, a stranger in the enemy's camp no less, had
renewed his faith. And there was no shortage of time for the
contemplation of divine interventions.

How long have I been imprisoned here in Antioch?
"Perhaps three months," he said aloud.

But how could he be sure?

Antonius' thoughts were interrupted by the soft footsteps of his guardian angel. Her silhouette appeared, and she began to lower the bucket, but when the bucket was halfway to the bottom, the girl seemed to startle. She hurriedly pulled the bucket back up. Something fell from the girl's hand in her rush. Antonius sighed heavily at his missed meal. He searched the ground to see if she had dropped something edible, but what he found instead was a ring. He brought the ring closer to his eyes to examine it in the dimness. It was small, silver, and had a single stone in the shape of a crescent moon. Turning it over in his fingers several times, Antonius wondered how many loaves of bread the ring would have fetched at the market in Byzantium.

Visions of the market and its endless stocks of fresh fish, meat, and fruits danced in his head. The fantasy was interrupted by a faint vibration. Opening his eyes, he stopped breathing and listened intently. Again, he sensed it. He placed his ear to the ground and waited. The small vibration gradually grew stronger, and after a few minutes, there was a distinct but still very minor rumble. Antonius was perplexed. The rumble grew louder still until he could feel it without his ear on the ground. The rumble was continuous and grew closer... closer...

"Horses!" he said aloud.

Before he could grasp what was happening, Antonius heard a tremendous crash echo down the hallway above the pit. Then came shouts and more crashes. Before long, there was the familiar sound of swords parrying and striking shields. The cacophony grew closer, and Antonius could hear two individual men above the pit. Soon their silhouettes came into view, and with a tremendous war cry, one forced the other over the edge. Antonius scrambled out of the way as the body of a Persian guard fell through the air to the ground next to him.

Frozen in disbelief, Antonius could hear the other man catching his breath.

He looked up from the bottom of the pit and shouted, "Hail, Roman!"

The other man stepped toward the pit and looked down. "Who is there?" came the reply in perfect Greek.

Antonius could barely contain his glee. "It is Antonius Andronicus, *pentarch* of Emperor Heraclius' vanguard, captured near Tarsus. Quickly! Bring me up from here while there is still Persian blood left to shed!"

* * *

When Antonius was dragged from the pit, several of the gathered soldiers performed the sign of the cross when they set eyes on his gaunt, bloody figure.

"Where are the others?" he demanded.

One of the men spoke up, "There was only one other Roman here."

"Who? Francio? Urbicus?"

"Francio."

"Take me to him."

The soldiers helped Antonius down the hallway into a large chamber he hadn't seen before. In it were several tables and barrels, as well as a dozen or so Roman officers and soldiers. Antonius caught sight of Francio sitting at one of the tables, his thin, bearded face devouring a haunch of lamb as a Roman physician tended to his wounds.

"Francio!"

"Antonius!"

The two men embraced as best they could in their poor conditions. Francio's normally handsome, vital face was withered. The angles of his cheekbones and temples were clearly visible through his thinned skin.

"It is good to see you alive," Antonius said, "where is Urbicus?"

Francio simply shook his head. Antonius' shoulders sank. They stood in silence for a long while before Antonius suddenly shouted in a rage and beat his fists upon the table.

He turned toward the others in the room and shouted again, "Where is that bastard Persian? The *argbadh* Ardashir! *Where*?"

An officer approached him and said, "One of their sentries must have alerted the garrison to our approach. When we arrived, there were only a few men remaining. The officers seem to have fled with the horses. They left their grain and arsenal behind."

"Well, why are we all standing here? Bring me a horse and sword!"

The men in the room stared, speechless. Francio quietly broke the silence, "Antonius. If you left now, the journey would be short. Sit. Eat. The time will come for vengeance. Now you must regain your strength."

The officer spoke again, "Francio is right. Roman *cataphracts* are hunting the cowards down as we speak, but our cavalrymen have overtaken our vanguards, and we don't know the strength of the Persian forces south of Antioch. Our men need to rest and eat as well."

Antonius beat his fists on the table again.

The men watched silently as Antonius composed himself and swore, "I don't care if it takes me until the day I die. With almighty God as my witness, I will strike that Persian down!"

Chapter II
On the Wings of the Desert Wind

    Asana gazed over her shoulder toward the distant
horizon at the conflagration consuming the city that had been
her home for many years. The austere barracks and military
quarters of Antioch were, in a sense, the only home she had
ever known. She had spent most of her earlier years living the
nomadic life of a commander's daughter. Her mother had died
in childbirth. Her father and elder brother were the only family
she had ever known, but now she did not even know if her
father was alive. Asana's life had been cast into the desert wind

and ground into dust under the hooves of Raucah, her loyal mare.

The horse was a long-suffering palomino *Akhal-Teke*, purchased by her father from a wealthy Kazakh merchant for the occasion of Asana's eleventh birthday. The majestic, golden sheen of the mare's coat inspired the young Asana to name the beast *Raucah*, meaning daylight in the Persian tongue. Asana kept three nightingale feathers she had collected from the banks of the Tigris during her childhood in Ctesiphon. Each time she groomed the mare, Asana meticulously braided these feathers back into Raucah's mane, just above the withers. The feathers were a rare constant in her life. Light enough to carry anywhere and durable enough to survive her nomadic life. She turned away from the sight of Antioch in flames and glanced down at those feathers, overcome by the situation.

She wept quietly while riding southward behind her brother, Bahram. There was no thought of returning to Antioch, and the sonorous water of the Tigris back in Ctesiphon seemed even more unreachable. She was adrift and found no solace in thoughts of the future.

"We will be fine, Asana. Father will send word to us once we reach Tyre. Then, when things have settled, he will send an escort to take us back."

Asana made no response. She loved her brother, but she could see that he was shaken by the surprise attack on the barracks. The truth was, neither of them knew what the future held or if their father was even still alive.

They rode through most of the first night, stopping only to water and rest the horses. They traveled always within sight of the coast, staying off the main roads. The frontier between the Roman and Persian empires shifted like the wind. A road that was safe one day could be enemy territory the next. Bahram was taking no chances with his younger sister's safety.

19

He knew that all of Syria and Judea were dangerous. Asana finally fell asleep in the saddle, and Bahram led Raucah by the reins. They reached the outskirts of Laodicea in the early morning.

Bahram woke Asana and instructed her to keep watch over the horses while he entered the city to purchase food. Asana led the horses to a rocky outcrop that kept them out of sight from three sides. As her brother marched off toward Laodicea, she began to take note of how hungry she was. The time since the attack in Antioch had been one unending maelstrom, and in such maelstroms, mundane worries like hunger often went unnoticed. She watched Bahram's figure recede in the distance as the sun dawned at his back.

The cool night air would soon be banished, and the desert heat would quickly make itself known. Asana sat on a flat boulder, drank from the waterskin, and waited, torturing herself by reliving the horrors of the previous day. She wept again at the thought of her father. They were bitter, futile tears filled with frustration. Was her beloved *Baba* alive? How long before she knew what fate had befallen him? Raucah nickered and nuzzled Asana's shoulder, and she turned and threw her arms around the mare's neck. It was a scene that had repeated itself throughout Asana's life. The young girl and her horse had developed a language that transcended mere words.

Bahram returned a few hours later carrying clothes. He placed the garments down and produced his saddle bag, from which he took dates, almonds, and olives. He handed Asana the food, and she began devouring the meal.

"I bought you simple clothes," he said. "It will be safer for the both of us if we dress like the Judeans."

Asana nodded, but she was too focused on eating to care.

After the humble meal, Asana and Bahram sat silently for some time.

Eventually, Asana asked, "Where do we go now?" Bahram sighed and didn't answer immediately. He was young still, and the sudden weight of the responsibility he now held furrowed his brow. She asked again, "Where?"

"I am not certain, Asana. We must end up in Tyre, no matter which route we take."

"I know that, but we cannot stay here much longer."

"You are right. But it will be safer to travel after sunset. It is too hot for the horses to travel now, and it will be more difficult for the Romans to find us after dark."

*　　*　　*

As the sun set over the sea, Bahram and Asana ate their evening meal and loaded their horses. Asana rubbed Raucah's muzzle and kissed her cheek before mounting the gentle beast. They set off southwards at a slow pace. If they went much faster, the people of Laodicea might think they were running from something. Then, when the Romans reached the city, the people would understand what they were running from. The Romans would offer silver to anyone who could assist in capturing the Persians who fled Antioch, and the people would be all too happy to oblige. Better to travel quietly and unnoticed.

As they meandered past Laodicea, Asana stared at the flickering lamps of the city in the distance and the darkness of the sea beyond. A cooling breeze had picked up, and the thick heat of the day had been blown out to sea. She took a deep breath, and for the first time in two days, she felt something resembling peace. She tilted her head back and marveled at the endless, jeweled sky. The constellation her father had shown her presented itself immediately: the seven stars of the *Parvin*.

She remembered the day her father first taught her about the stars. She had sat on *Baba's* lap, and he pointed up toward the *Parvin*.

"Do you see that, Asana? Those beautiful stars? When the Ahura Mazda *created the world, he knew we mortals were forgetful, so he made the* Parvin *bright in the sky to remind us."*

"Remind us of what, Baba?"

"Remind us of the Amesha Spenta.*"*

"What is the Amesha Spenta?*"*

"It is the seven ways the Ahura wants us to be. Creative, devoted, purposeful, disciplined, whole, truthful, and immortal."

"I don't understand, Baba."

"You are young still, beloved Asana. You will understand these things more with every season. But they are up there in the sky for you to see whenever you wish!"

Bahram interrupted her reminiscence. "We should speed up now until we reach Gabala." They brought the horses to a canter, and Asana focused on her riding and the terrain in front of her. "We won't stop in when we reach the town. There is a river further south. We will bring the horses there to water."

"Good," she replied.

The landscape unfolded before her like a dream. Endless sand, tangled brush, and towering palms, all glowing in the moonlight. There was the smell of salt in the air and the rhythm of Raucah's hooves. It was hypnotizing, but Asana knew she must stay awake. Twice before they reached Gabala, they encountered men on camels heading north toward Laodicea. The siblings hid behind brush and palms to avoid being seen. When they remounted after stopping for the second time, Bahram was nearly thrown from the saddle. His horse had been spooked by a snake. He brought his mount under control quickly, but he noticed that Asana was spooked as well.

"At least it wasn't a Roman snake..." he said with soft laughter.

Asana smiled. Bahram was very conscious of his sister. With their mother dead and their father being shuffled all around the empire, he had always felt responsible for his younger sibling. Asana knew this and appreciated his efforts to assuage her anxiety. He was only twenty years of age, but he did his best to seem older and more capable for Asana's peace of mind. But both he and Asana understood how precarious the situation was. They were alone in a land that was not theirs, pursued by Roman cavalry. Any missteps could mean their capture. Or worse.

Gabala appeared on the horizon, and as they approached, they slowed the horses to a walk. They stayed even further away than they did when passing Laodicea. Travelers this late in the evening always arouse suspicion. The city came and went.

Bahram commented, "It's a shame. I hear there is a beautiful amphitheater in Gabala. I would have liked to have seen it."

They kicked the horses to a canter again and rode on.

After what seemed like an eternity, they reached the river Bahram had spoken of. They dismounted and led the horses to the banks, where they dipped their heads and drank furiously. Asana filled the waterskins and washed up in the river. The cool water was rejuvenating, and it brought calmness to her mind. Bahram led the horses a few hundred paces from the river to a pine grove.

Here, he handed Asana more almonds and dates, saying, "Eat and then sleep. We won't have much time. The dawn is coming, and others will come to the river for water."

She lay on the ground, staring up at the *Parvin,* reminded of how much she missed her father, and slowly drifted off to sleep…

* * *

…She dreamt of an endless desert and of a river, but when she approached, the river receded, replaced by the cackling visage of a djinni*. The* djinni *twisted and whirled, then burst into sand and was carried away by the wind. When the sand cleared, the river was gone. In its place, there was a city that looked much like Antioch. She marched towards it, but the cackling* djinni *reappeared, hovering over the city like a cloud. She looked on in horror as the apparition erupted into flame and fell onto the rooftops of the buildings as a thousand embers, setting the city ablaze. She turned and ran, leaving the charred city behind.*

Next, she came upon a gleaming oasis. Sprouting amongst the palms of the oasis were flowers of impossible richness. Butterflies and songbirds of all kinds flitted between the trees. She was in awe. She looked toward the shade at the water's edge and saw a man crouched, bringing water onto his face and neck. His back had many scars. She could not recognize him, so she stepped forward. The man stood silently and slowly. But as soon as he began to turn his face toward her, the cackling djinni *rose from the sand and grabbed her by the arms…*

"Get up!" Bahram said in a stern whisper as he shook his sister awake.

As Asana sat up, he placed a hand over her mouth and pointed toward the river. She turned her head, but her eyes were still adjusting to the sunlight. Through the pines, she saw the glint of the sun off of a bronze helmet. Her jaw dropped. Six Roman soldiers were watering their horses on the

24

riverbank. The siblings untied and mounted the horses as quietly as they could and made their way east. As soon as they were out of sight, they trotted. And as soon as Bahram thought they couldn't be heard, they took the horses to a full gallop.

Where they could, Bahram took them into the water on the riverbank to disguise their tracks. It was a long while before they allowed themselves to slow.

Out of breath, Bahram said, "We need to cross, and we cannot rest until we get to Tyre." They found a shallow crossing, and they let the horses drink their fill on the other side. "We will make it, Asana. We will be tired, but we will make it."

"I know," Asana replied half-heartedly. They set off southward, this time well out of sight of the coast. They made steady progress, but the ride through the heat of day was difficult for the horses. Several hours had passed, and Raucah, who was typically very forgiving of Asana's demands, began to squeal and grunt in protest of the difficult ride. "If we don't set the horses in shade, they won't make it to Tyre."

Bahram sighed. He knew his sister was right. Asana was a natural equestrienne, and she had proven her intuition with horses to him time and time again. Over the next ridge, they were able to see a stand of cedars in the distance.

Bahram lifted his chin toward the trees. "There. With any luck, there will be water as well."

They reached the cedars and tied the horses. Asana thought the horses seemed agitated, and Bahram had noticed as well. Asana removed their saddles and rubbed their chins and muzzles, whispering in a sing-song voice into their ears. Bahram looked about for signs of a well or spring, but he knew it was unlikely.

"There is no water here," he said directly.

Asana uncapped one of the waterskins and drank, then handed it to her brother, who also drank. Then she placed it on the ground in front of Raucah. The mare dipped her head and lapped the water from the mouth of the waterskin. She did the same for her brother's horse.

Suddenly, Raucah squealed and reared, backing up, but was unable to get free of her tie. Bahram's horse shrieked and bolted. The horse had broken free of its line and set off at a full gallop. Asana and Bahram looked at each other, equally startled. They turned and were struck motionless. Standing thirty paces away was a lioness staring directly at them. As they stared back, the corners of the beast's mouth receded, revealing glistening fangs. This frightening display was accompanied by a low, slow growl that chilled them both. Bahram had laid his spear against one of the cedars along with his saddlebag. He cursed himself for not keeping his weapon close at hand.

Asana was frozen in place. Raucah was struggling against her tie as Bahram edged toward his spear. In a flash, the lioness set off and pounced on Bahram. He grabbed his spear and turned just in time to see the fearsome beast leap through the air. He was able to bring his weapon around, and the spearpoint pierced the lioness' shoulder just as the full weight of the animal was falling on him. The spear splintered as he fell backward to the ground, and he felt claws tearing at his side. The teeth that were aiming for his neck instead sunk into his shoulder. But the lioness was chastened by the spear wound and slunk away, bleeding heavily.

The whole episode was over in a moment.

Asana ran to her brother, saying, "No! No, no, no…"

Bahram was breathing heavily. He managed to say quietly, "I will… be fine, Asana."

She grabbed the waterskin and rinsed his wounds. The flesh on his side was torn, and his shoulder and chest had been punctured by the cat's teeth. Asana tore her garment, bandaged the cuts as best she could, and propped him against a tree out of the sunlight.

Bahram's horse had run off with the food and all of Bahram's belongings, and they were still nearly a hundred miles from Tyre. Asana knew they would have to start out again soon. The food was already gone, and the water would not last.

"You will have... to go on... without me, Asana."

"Don't be foolish, Bahram. We will both make it to Tyre, and we will find a doctor there."

"Asana, you are not... going to make it... to Tyre with me... slowing you down. Leave me."

"Quiet! You are coming with me. We are leaving once Raucah is rested and the sun begins to set."

And that was that. Asana typically deferred to her older brother, who had looked out for her so well for so long. But when she needed to have her way, she could be as stubborn and assertive as anyone Bahram had ever met. So, when a few hours passed and the sun began to sink in the western sky, they departed. Asana helped her brother up. Bahram groaned and winced as they maneuvered him into Raucah's saddle.

Asana mounted and whispered in her beloved mare's ear, "This will be a long ride, girl. But we have to do it!"

Raucah snorted.

* * *

They rode straight through the evening and into the early morning once more. Asana periodically turned to give Bahram water from the skin. She was consuming as little for herself as possible. They had gone off course after fleeing from the Romans near the river.

Bahram weakly lifted his arm and pointed, managing to whisper, "There."

His voice was a soft rasp. Asana gave him more water and then led Raucah in the direction Bahram pointed. The horse was faltering, and Asana dismounted to relieve the burden. She gave Raucah a drink from the waterskin and then led her by the halter.

After several more arduous miles on foot, they reached a second river just as the sun was peering over the eastern horizon. The slow, meandering river was in a shallow valley. There was no one, Roman or Syrian, in sight. Bahram barely had the strength to sit up, so Asana led him down to a tall cypress near the water. She helped him out of the saddle and sat him against the trunk of the tree. His bandages had soaked through with blood, and his breathing was labored. Asana filled the waterskin from the river and rushed back to her brother. He could only manage a small sip.

She washed his forehead and hands. "I will go search for some roots to eat..." she offered desperately.

"No! Stay..."

She felt tears welling in her eyes. "Bahram..."

"It is... all right, Asana. You will... make it to Tyre without me."

"Bahram, no..."

"Y-yes!" he sputtered. "Yes. You will... go south until you... reach the next river... follow it west... it will take you toward Tripoli... go after nightfall... and find food. Then head south... through old Berytus... to Tyre... Find a Persian... Persian officer and tell them... tell them what happened." Bahram coughed weakly.

"I am not going to leave you here!"

"You must, Asana."

"Then I will come back for you!" Asana insisted.

Her brother simply smiled and set his eyes toward the riverbank. "Look," he said, "Persian lilies...." Asana turned and beheld the deep crimson and purple bells of the lilies growing near the water. Their vibrant color shamed the sullen hues of the desert around them. "Our mother... loved... Persian lilies. She would pick them... near the river... would hang them... over the door." He grimaced in pain before continuing. "I wish... I wish you could have... known her."

Asana wept.

Bahram did his best to smile through his pain again. "You will make it... little sister. South to the River... to Tripoli... to Berytus... then Tyre." He coughed weakly. "I...wish you... could... have known... her." With another weak cough, his body shivered and gave way.

Asana had no words and no thoughts. Only the feeling of complete and utter abandonment. Her soul had been cast into desolation and was now damned to wander there alone. Her sorrowful cries rang out, seeming out of place amongst the chattering of the birds and the babbling of the river. She stayed with Bahram for a long time, unable to bring herself to leave. Her older brother, her protector, was gone forever. It was a reality too difficult to accept. She went down to the riverbank and pulled some of the Persian lilies. She brought them back and placed them in Bahram's lifeless grip, placed his hands on his lap, and shut his eyes.

Another wave of mournful dread wracked her heart as she did so. *How can I possibly go on alone?* She knelt down next to her brother, despondent and stricken. Then a nightingale landed on the ground not far from her and sang a most curious song. It was the same song she had heard a thousand times from a thousand other nightingales. But at the same time, it differed completely from anything she had ever heard before. Different in an intangible, unmistakable way. The bird made two little hops toward Asana and seemed to look right at her, singing again before flying away southward across the river.

A nightingale! Of all birds…

The omen was enough to push her onward. She brought Raucah to the water to drink, filled her waterskin, and mounted. She turned one last time as she crossed the river to look at Bahram. He was at final rest under the cypress, surrounded by chattering songbirds and clasping lilies in his hands.

I will make it, brother.

*   *   *

Most of the day had already passed, and Asana had fallen asleep in the saddle twice. How long had she been awake? *It doesn't matter,* she concluded. Once the sun sank, she felt somewhat invigorated. She pressed on, pushing her horse while the air was cooler. She reached the next river before daybreak. After letting Raucah graze and drink, Asana tied her off and found a spot to lay amongst some tall grasses. She desperately needed sleep, but the hunger made it difficult.

After resting as well as she could, she set off westward down the river, just as Bahram had instructed. It was midday, but she needed food and could not wait. She could not let her guard down. The Romans would follow the coast roads south, and they could be anywhere by now. After following the track of the river for many hours, she caught her first glimpse of Tripoli in the distance as the sun was setting. Asana decided that it might attract less attention if she approached on foot, so she tied Raucah to a cedar on the outskirts of the city. She had no particular plan. She was now driven only by the emptiness in her stomach.

She could smell the salt air of the sea as she approached, saddlebag in hand. But mixed with the salt air was another smell... familiar to her. *Oranges!* Asana remembered that mules and camels laden with oranges, dates, almonds, and figs would come to Antioch from the south. The merchants arriving from Tripoli always had oranges with them. As she walked further downriver, the orchards came into view. Row after glorious row of orange trees, fruiting and rustling in the breeze.

She rushed toward the tree closest to her, practically skipping on the way. The famished girl plucked an orange and tore into it ravenously. The first bite was pure relief. She made quick work of the orange and plucked another one. Asana bit into the second as she plucked several more and dropped them into her saddlebag. There were a few stone buildings toward the end of the row of trees: the farmer's house and storehouse, most likely. She made her way toward the buildings as the last remnants of light drained from the sky.

As she approached, the clatter of ceramic and muffled conversation spilled out the window of the farmhouse, along with the tantalizing smell of cooked meat. *They are eating supper.* Asana quietly stepped toward the other building, hoping to find another kind of food to bring with her. She had to fight to suppress her guilt about taking from the farmer. The *Ahura Mazda* would certainly frown upon such an act. But she was desperate, and she needed something more substantial than oranges to nourish her if she was going to finish the journey. She knew the closer she got to the city center, the riskier the search for food would become. The other building was indeed a storehouse, and inside, amongst the tools and straw, were many amphorae lined up against opposite walls. She removed the lid from several and found them empty.

Her heart sank, and she began to leave. But at the last moment, she decided to search the opposite wall and opened one of the amphorae there. It was full. She grabbed a handful of the contents and brought them to her eyes to examine in the fading light. Almonds! She put the almonds in with the oranges. In the next Amphora, she found pistachios, and in the next, chickpeas. She put a few handfuls of each into her saddlebag. *That should be plenty,* she thought. *The farmer won't even notice anything is gone.*

But when she looked up again, she was startled. An old man holding a lantern stood at the doorway to the storehouse, staring directly at her.

"*G'ana'ba!*" he barked.

Asana had overheard enough of the merchants in Antioch speaking Aramaic to know that '*g'ana'ba*' meant thief. He approached Asana, who was frozen with fear, opened her saddlebag, and looked inside.

"*G'ana'ba,*" he said again, roughly pulling the saddlebag out of her hands. "*Aa'rp'ea,*" he said, pointing outside. Asana did not move. The man repeated louder, "*Aa'rp'ea!*"

Asana understood the message, but as she was working up the courage to move, an old woman appeared next to the man in the doorway. She had a motherly, concerned expression on her face that softened as she beheld Asana. She turned to the man and spoke to him quietly. *Husband and wife,* Asana thought. The old man responded to the woman and gestured with his big, calloused hands. Asana heard him say "*g'ana'ba*" again and watched as he showed the old woman the saddlebag and its contents. The old woman replied to him in a softer tone and gestured toward Asana.

When the old woman finished speaking, the old man's shoulders dropped. He took a deep breath, let out a long sigh, and motioned for Asana to follow them outside. After she followed them out, the man handed her the saddlebag and bowed his head. The old woman embraced her husband's hand and smiled warmly at Asana. She then traced a cross on her own forehead with her right thumb. *Christians...* Asana realized. She clasped her hands and bowed deeply to the couple, then scampered back through the orange orchard, feeling as grateful as she ever had.

* * *

Raucah nickered gleefully when she noticed that Asana was approaching. Asana was equally gleeful, throwing her arms around the mare's neck and kissing her cheek. She pulled an orange from the saddlebag, peeled it, and fed it to the horse, who devoured it in a single bite. Raucah pawed at the ground restlessly.

"I know, I know! I just need some water, and we are off."

She filled the waterskin, untied and mounted the horse, then crossed the river headed southward.

This was the last leg of the journey, but it was also the longest. She would have to camp in the open at least once before she reached Tyre. Asana made good time staying within sight of the old Roman imperial road but not daring to travel on it. She feasted on nuts, chickpeas, and oranges along the way. More than once, she caught herself looking up at the sky, mesmerized by the majesty of it all. And more than once, she wept at the thought of Bahram at rest under the cypress.

Asana was able to pull herself out of her grief only by distracting herself with the situation at hand. She had to stay alert. Visions of lions and snakes and Romans on horseback paraded through her mind's eye as she pressed on...

* * *

She came upon the ruins of Berytus in the morning. Bahram had told her that the city was destroyed by an earthquake and a giant wave many years ago. Most of the people had left for other cities, and all that was left was the stone wreckage of the ancient buildings. The scene was quite haunting. The muttering of the sea in the distance and the wind echoing down through the ruins were the only sounds to be heard. Raucah snorted nervously, and her ears pointed forward as they reached the remains of a road heading through the city.

Asana slowed down, stroked the horse's neck, and said soothingly, "There's nothing here, girl." She looked around at the rows of fallen buildings and spoke again, "Nothing here at all...."

She was persuading herself as much as her horse because, despite her words, there was an ominous feeling that there *might* be *something* here. After wandering for a bit, she found a place where she felt she could rest: a stone house that had three walls that were mostly intact. They would not be easily seen, and it would provide shelter from the sun. She led Raucah in, dismounted, and ate a quick meal from her saddlebag. Before long, the bag was under her head, and she was fast asleep.

Asana awoke on her back in darkness. A million stars greeted her eyes as she opened them. *I slept through the whole day!* Nervously, she sat up. Raucah was right where Asana had left her, grazing near one of the stone walls of the ruined house. The mare nickered at Asana as she roused.

"Hello, girl. I suppose I was more exhausted than I realized."

Asana walked over to the horse and rubbed her muzzle before stepping out of the ruined house. She surveyed the city around her, which seemed even more barren at night. But a glint in the distance caught her eye. It was a fire.

Her curiosity drove her towards it like a moth, although she had many second thoughts. Walking as softly as she could down ruined roadways and through rubble in the darkness, she kept her eyes glued to the warm glow of the flames. At last, she reached a crumbling wall on a small hill. She crouched for the final few paces and peered cautiously through a cleft in the wall.

She could see down to the bottom of the hill, where there was a firepit lined with stones. The small, crackling fire was spinning a yarn of smoke that was pulled toward the sea by the steady, gentle breeze. Near the fire was a ragged blanket, and there were all manner of things on it that Asana couldn't quite make out. She squinted, trying to get a better view, when a voice rang out behind her.

"*Sh'lam lek!*"

Asana nearly jumped out of her skin. She was now sitting on the ground, trying to back away, but she was still up against the stone wall.

"*Sh'lam lek. Al tira.*"

Asana held her breath as she observed who had spoken. A short, old woman with long white hair stood just an arm's length away from her. In her left hand was a gnarled walking staff, knobby like the knuckles that gripped it. And in her right hand, she carried a hare by its ears.

The woman's gaze never wavered from Asana. "*Ana sha'lah b'shlamek?*"

"I'm sorry, I do not speak much Aramaic…" Asana explained.

"Well, lucky for us, I speak Persian!" the woman answered. Her voice had a slight hoarseness. She spoke quietly, but her words carried a certain weight. "Come! You must be hungry after your long nap."

She must have seen me while I was sleeping, Asana realized. She was too taken aback to protest, so she followed the old woman past the crumbling wall and down the hill to the campfire.

"Please sit," the woman ordered gently.

Asana sat and watched as the woman picked up a small iron cauldron, hanging it over the fire using her walking staff.

The old woman gutted the hare with a small obsidian blade she had on her blanket. Then she skinned it and tossed it into the cauldron whole. She picked up a piece of canvas and unfolded it, producing all manner of greens and roots, which she promptly threw in with the hare. The old woman held her hands to the fire and murmured a few words in Aramaic before turning toward Asana.

She looked up and down and then stared at Asana's eyes for a long moment before asking, "What is your name, child?"

"Asana."

"Asana… And where do you come from, Asana?"

"I was born in Ctesiphon, on the Tigris."

"You are many miles from Ctesiphon."

"I am on my way to Tyre. I was only stopping here to rest. I thought I would be alone."

"Yes. I watched you ride in this morning. You have a clever horse."

Asana smiled. "I do. It was a gift from my father."

"And where is your father?"

Asana's smile faded. "I really do not know."

"Hmm."

"I hope to hear from him once I reach Tyre."

"I see."

Asana studied the lines on the woman's face. The shadows cast by the firelight accentuated the deep furrows in her brow. "And you... what is your name?"

It was the old woman's turn to smile. "My mother called me Maren, although it has been many years since anyone has said that name."

"And where do you come from?"

"Here."

"Here? In Berytus?"

"Yes."

"But I have heard that this city has been abandoned for decades."

"Yes. It is true. I was born here before the sea swallowed the city."

"And you did not leave?"

"No..." The old woman, once called Maren, took a deep breath and gazed into the fire before continuing, "One morning, my mother sent me east into the foothills to gather. While I was plucking herbs, the ground shook mightily, and I watched as the sea climbed out of itself and swept the city away. There were not many people left. I never saw my mother again. Many of the survivors moved to Sidon. Those of us who stayed started to rebuild, but the task was too much. Most gave up hope and left, following the others to Sidon, and of the few that remained, I am the only one left."

"How sorrowful," said Asana.

"Well, some fortunes are cast more sorrowfully than others. It has always been this way."

They sat in silence for some time, and Maren stirred the stew cooking over the fire. The smell wafting from the cauldron made Asana salivate. It seemed like forever since she had eaten a full, warm meal. Maren reached over to her blanket and grabbed two small ceramic bowls. She poured the contents of the cauldron into the two bowls and handed one to her guest. Asana thanked her, brought the stew up to her nose, and inhaled. She let her hands warm for a moment on the bowl before taking a sip.

She could not have asked for a more perfect and invigorating meal. Maren saw how quickly the girl devoured the stew and offered her more, which she gratefully accepted. When Asana had eaten her fill, she leaned backward and cast her eyes up towards the stars. And as she did, a glimmer appeared in the sky: a shooting star. It painted a streak of light and was gone in an instant.

Asana put her hand over her heart and quietly expressed her amazement. "My!"

"Hm?"

"It was a shooting star," Asana explained. "But it makes me wonder. Am I the only one who saw it? And if I had not looked up at this very moment, I would not have seen it at all. Was I meant to see it?"

Maren smiled, and Asana could see a glimmer in her eye that matched the shooting star. "That is the question, isn't it?"

"But there is no answer, is there?"

Maren breathed in deeply and exhaled slowly, as if weighing her thoughts. "I am not sure it is a question that has an answer. But it *is* a question that provides a choice." She reached behind her and brought a few pieces of wood into the fire before continuing, "You see, there are two paths a person can take. One is to choose to see everything as an accident, to place no particular importance on auspicious timings and coincidence, and to view the world as a place of chaos dominated by the individual will.

"The other path is to choose to see the world as a place of meaning, where the universe conspires to whisper its secrets in your ear when no one else is watching, a place of order dominated by the divine will.

"To choose the first path is to choose a path that can be empowering and full of temporary pleasures but ultimately leads to a place of emptiness. To choose the second path is to choose a path that can be full of hardship and sacrifice but ultimately leads to a place of fulfillment. And sometimes, when following this second path, one might even stumble upon a glimpse of the divine plan…."

Asana was struck by the old woman's words. She took some time to digest it all before inquiring, "Are you saying that one can see into the future?"

"Oh, I would not say it is possible to see into the future. Only that sometimes one can feel which way the wind is blowing and *know what must come to pass….*"

At that very moment, the breeze picked up, bending and dimming the fire in front of Asana, who felt a chill envelop her whole body. There was a gravity in the old woman's eyes that Asana was only now noticing.

Asana stammered, "You… you are a…"

"A sorceress? A witch? I have heard it all before, child. And when I see such fear, I am reminded of why I chose to remain here amongst these ruins, alone. Tell me, do you believe that I harbor any ill-will toward you?"

"No," Asana answered directly. "And I am sorry. I was just startled. I am not used to being in the wilderness alone."

"Well, after about sixty years, you become accustomed to it!" Maren laughed heartily at her own joke. "But then again, this place was my home," she said, motioning to the remnants of the city around them. She sighed heavily as she looked out upon the ghostly scenery. "Go on, child. You must set out for Tyre, and your horse is getting hungry."

Asana did not protest. The old woman was right. She stood up to leave and thanked the old woman. As she stepped away, the same curiosity that drove her towards the campfire drove her to turn and face the old woman, who was gathering her belongings into her blanket.

"Maren..."

"Hm?"

"Do you think you... Will you tell me what must come to pass for me?"

Maren froze, then turned towards Asana. Her eyes narrowed as she measured the girl's intentions. "Once such a thing is told, it cannot be untold. Perhaps it would be better to find out for yourself."

"Please, Maren, I want to hear it."

Maren grumbled and reluctantly reached towards the now-dying fire. She took some ash from the firepit and rubbed her hands together before muttering some words under her breath. She walked over to Asana and grabbed her by the wrists. Maren looked into Asana's eyes for a long while and then up at the sky. Finally, she rubbed her ashen hands into Asana's palms before running her fingers along the lines she found there.

She released Asana's hands and shook her head before speaking, "You have looked upon your true love and not known him once. So you shall do so a second time, still not knowing. And fate is cruel. For when you finally see, it will be through bittersweet eyes, for the end will not be far off!"

Chapter III
The Fortunes

More than a week had passed, and the fires that had been set during the fighting had long since burned out. Antonius felt some of his strength returning, although his experience in prison had aged him beyond his years. The wounds on his back had finally begun to heal. And with the help of regular meals and regular trips to the famous Roman baths of Antioch, he would soon be fit enough to travel with the vanguards again.

While he convalesced, Roman horsemen would return to the city with news of a Persian captured or killed. Each time, Antonius would ask if anyone had found Ardashir or his snake, Narseh. So far, the answer had been no.

One horseman even informed Antonius, "You have asked so many of the horsemen that one could no longer travel the imperial roads without overhearing talk about the two Persians and the Roman *pentarch* who wants their heads."

"I will find them," was Antonius' terse reply.

He had been waiting patiently for Emperor Heraclius' decision to march either south or east. Soon, he could wait no longer. He made himself such a nuisance to the officers of the Antioch garrison that they agreed to let him venture out with a vanguard simply to be rid of him. Before he left, he stopped by Francio's quarters to speak with his friend. He had regained some of his weight, and the color had returned to his skin. His familiar handsomeness and his jovial countenance had also returned, though Antonius couldn't help but notice he looked far older now.

"Francio, are you well?"

"Well enough, my friend."

"I will be heading southward in the morning with a vanguard in search of the men who kept us here. Will you join me?"

"You are mad, Antonius. You are not even healed."

"I am healed enough to hunt Persians, Francio."

"You would do Emperor Heraclius a great service by staying and joining the next offensive against Hieropolis and Edessa."

"But I would do the world an even greater service by ridding it of Ardashir and that swine lieutenant of his."

"I would like to see them gone as well, Antonius. And if Urbicus' voice could pierce the gloom of the burial grounds, he would agree. But that does not mean that this is the path you should take."

"This is the path I *will* take. And that path begins at daybreak."

"I will pray for you, Antonius."

"Pray for Ardashir because his soul will stand at the altar of judgment before mine!"

The following morning, Antonius met with the Master of Camp. The *stratopedarches* had laid out the water, food, and weaponry for the vanguard. Four men volunteered to accompany Antonius, and each was given a spear, a sword, a bow, a helmet, and five days' rations. Antonius led the men to a shrine that the Romans had set up in the prison. They knelt before the icon on the altar and prayed for good fortune. Antonius made sure to ask for his forgiveness in advance. With their deference to the almighty properly demonstrated, the men walked to the stables and readied their horses.

When they were all mounted, Antonius turned to the men and spoke, "We are going south along the imperial road, and we will go all the way to Alexandria in Egypt if we must. We will kill or capture any of the Persians we find that were scattered by the assault on Antioch. We will bring back any and all information we gather that will assist Emperor Heraclius as he marches on towards Ctesiphon. And, as I am sure you have heard, I am looking for two Persians in particular. I consider it a matter of honor, and I am grateful to all of you for your assistance."

One of the men spoke up, "It is *our* honor, sir."

Antonius bowed his head humbly, and the five men rode southward out of Antioch.

* * *

Asana arrived in Tyre when the moon was full. She crossed the great stone causeway to the walled city under its cool light. Now the moon was a thin crescent, and there had still been no word from her father. In fact, there had been no word from any Persian. The Persian officers that Bahram had expected to be in Tyre were nowhere to be found. From what Asana had gathered from the locals, the Persian troops once stationed here had set off toward Damascus and Palmyra when they heard that the Romans were advancing through Pontus. She had hit a dead end.

The morning after she reached Tyre, it became clear that she was in a bind. With no Persian officers to speak to, no place to stay, and no money, Asana was short on choices. She went down to the forum, where the merchants had set up their stalls. Most of the people in the forum spoke Greek, and unlike Aramaic, it was a language that Asana knew quite well. After approaching several of the merchants and vendors, she found one who was willing to purchase her saddle.

Asana was not really in a position to negotiate, and so she parted with the saddle, reins, and halter for two hundred silver *denarii*. With this windfall, she paid an innkeeper for a place for her and Raucah to stay. And she did stay—on a humble hay bed at the inn—for almost two weeks. She was quickly running out of silver. Soon she would have no money, no place to stay, nowhere to go, and no saddle to sell.

Each day she ate a small meal at the inn and then returned to the forum, where she eavesdropped on whoever had arrived in Tyre most recently. She was hoping to hear some piece of news that would help her figure out what to do next. The gossip she overheard, however, was vague and often contradictory. One traveler claimed that the Romans had been pushed back out of Antioch, but then the next traveler claimed that the Romans had garrisoned Antioch and were marching on Palmyra.

44

Never had Asana felt so frustrated. She was like a ship without a sail, drifting, just waiting to be dashed upon the shoals. A crossroads was rapidly approaching. Her situation was untenable, and a decision would have to be made. She had no means to stay but nowhere to go. At last, she broke. She decided she would set off toward Damascus in the hopes that she would find a Persian officer there. Then she could explain who she was and see if anyone had heard where the *argbadh* of Antioch was currently.

It was an unlikely plan, but it was the only hope that she could summon. So, with her remaining few *denarii,* Asana purchased fruit and bread in preparation for the journey. She filled her waterskin and let Raucah have her fill from the well behind the inn.

Asana rubbed Raucah's muzzle and spoke softly to her, "We have no saddle this time, girl, so this is not going to be fun for either of us. But we can take our time because I think those Romans would have given up by now, wherever they are."

Raucah snorted. Asana walked the horse through the streets of Tyre until she reached the stone archway at the edge of the city. Here she mounted.

She looked down at the nightingale feathers braided into Raucah's mane. "Sorry, girl, these are going to get in the way."

She unbraided the feathers and threaded them through the thongs in her bangle. Asana wrapped her fingers around the horse's mane and set off into the desert.

She made her way along the dusty trail and passed a few others heading into Tyre. Several miles into her journey, as the road wound through some boulders strewn on the desert floor, she was startled by a man dressed in rags. He was sitting up against the bottom of one of the boulders. Asana was not sure if he was asleep or dead.

"Hello..." she ventured. The figure stirred weakly. "Are you ok?"

A whisper was all the man could manage. She dismounted, grabbed her waterskin, and offered it. The man nodded weakly. She brought it to him and poured some into his mouth, which he happily accepted.

But then Asana noticed a curious glint in the man's eye, and a villainous smile cracked across his face. Without warning, she heard a loud smack, and Raucah shrieked and bolted down the road back toward Tyre. When she turned to see what had scared her horse, there was a giant of a man looking back at her.

Her stomach sank as it dawned on her what was happening.

The man on the ground stood and laughed heartily to himself. "Thank you very much for the water, my dear. It was very generous of you. Now, if you would please follow me, you will be coming with us."

Asana didn't waste any time before attempting to run back toward Tyre after Raucah, but the giant ended her escape before it could begin, pushing her to the ground.

Asana groaned as the dust kicked up into her face, and her palms were cut on the rocky sand. She felt the giant man's massive hand clamp on her nape, and he pulled her up from the ground with one arm. She struggled, but the giant simply tightened his grip, and she gave up, fearing her bones might break. The giant dragged her around the boulders to where a covered cart was waiting.

The shorter man approached Asana and spoke, "It would be so much easier for all of us if you had not done such a foolish thing. I am afraid I will have to use rope now..."

The two brutes bound Asana's wrists and ankles with rope. They shoved cloth into her mouth and pulled a canvas sack over her head and shoulders. She was tossed into the back of the covered cart.

"Now, be sure not to make any noise. Otherwise, my friend here will make you regret your disobedience. Besides, as far as anyone knows, you are simply an escaped slave being returned to her master."

The giant grabbed hold of the cart handles and began marching back toward Tyre as the other followed. Asana's heart was racing, and she could barely compose herself.

There are times in every life when plans are cast aside, and the needs and urgency of the moment dwarf all other considerations. They are times of danger and uncertainty where a long future is not necessarily promised. They are times when the mind is cruelly trapped in the present, without the luxury of daydreams or hope. These times descended like a vulture on the poor young girl from Ctesiphon, picking clean the last bit of flesh from the bones of her former life. She had no hope of escaping now, and even if she did, she would not make it very far without Raucah. She resigned herself to her fate. For the moment.

Asana could hear the noises of the city as they approached: distant shouts and chatter and the plodding of horse and camel hooves. She listened intently, waiting for any indication of an opportunity to escape. She wrenched her arms against the ropes, but they were well tied and did not give. Soon, she could hear the sound of water, and she felt the cart wheels rolling over wooden planks. They were at the docks in Tyre. The giant placed the cart down and pulled her out, throwing Asana over his shoulder. He proceeded to walk up the gangplank of a ship moored at the dock. With no fanfare or delay, he took his prisoner below deck and placed her in an iron cage.

Asana heard the loud clang of the iron door as it was being shut. She heard her captors walk off, leaving her tied in the darkness in the hold of the ship. She struggled mightily once more against her ropes and fumbled about uselessly for something—anything that might help her liberate herself from her wretched situation. She shouted in frustration and eventually resigned herself to tears. The hold of the ship was much cooler than the desert air, and after a while, the gentle rocking of the boat had a mesmerizing effect. Exhausted, pained, and with no tears left to cry, she fell at last into a deep sleep.

*　*　*

The Roman horsemen had made several days' journey south but had so far found nothing. No Ardashir, no Narseh, no Persians at all. While the other men expected to conduct a somewhat routine reconnaissance, Antonius had placed no such limitations on the journey. He would find the Persians even if he had to ride through the gates of hell itself, and he would kill them with his own hands.

At a river south of Gabala, the men came across a man slumped against a cypress, dead. His hands were clasped across withered flowers.

"A Persian," one of the men stated. "Young."

"Yes," Antonius replied, "and unless he was picking flowers when he died, he was with at least one other."

The soldier pointed toward the wounds on the body. "He was mauled. No tracks, man or beast. Whoever he was with is several days gone at least."

Antonius nodded. There was something curiously peaceful about the dead Persian, something authentically human that briefly pierced Antonius' vengeful resolve. Perhaps it was the withered flowers in the dead man's grasp, or maybe it was the expression of pure grief that was now forever carved on his face. Whoever this young Persian was, he had truly had something to live for. Antonius' stoic detachment had lapsed as he dwelled on the dead man, but his mind soon returned to his mission, and he motioned for his men to continue southward. They watered their horses and set off into the desert heat.

Towards evening, they reached Tripoli and rode through the center of the city. The residents approached the Romans, offering food, cloth, and all manner of things for purchase.

Antonius put up his hand and spoke to the crowd in Greek, "Friends! My men will be purchasing food at a fair price from many of you, but there is something I value more than all the oranges in Tripoli. If any of you have knowledge of any Persian officers who have passed through this city recently, I am willing to pay *one hundred silver denarii* to hear what you know."

His offer sent the gathered crowd into an uproar. Every hand seemed to reach out, and shouts about Persians of all kinds filled the street.

Antonius leaned over to the man on his flank and said with a smile, "Silver seems to be good for the memory."

"It may be even better for the imagination," came his Roman comrade's reply.

Antonius and his men listened to the claims of the townspeople one by one. Some said they saw Persians heading east. Some said they saw a few Persians embark on a cargo ship on their way to Alexandria. None provided any information of use to the Romans. The sun was setting, and the men were losing patience with the people. Antonius noticed an old man squatting against the stone foundation of the building on the other side of the road, staring at him.

Separating himself from the crowd and from his men, Antonius marched straight toward the old man. He was skin and bones, and his ratty beard reached his navel. His knobbed knees and gnarled fingers told a tale of a life spent working in the fields and orchards.

As Antonius approached, he asked, "Old man, do you understand Greek?" The old man nodded but motioned to his own throat and shook his head. "You are mute..."

The old man nodded again.

Antonius squatted beside the old man and spoke quietly toward his ear, "I am here looking for a few men who fled from Antioch. Have you seen any Persians pass through Tripoli?"

The old man looked into Antonius' eyes and, acknowledging nothing, looked away again.

Antonius stood. "Surely you remember the Romans have been friends of Tripoli since you were a young boy. They brought peace to this land and allowed the citizens to eat from their own orchards. But the Persians have brought nothing but suffering and destruction. Old man, if you have seen the Persians, it is for the good of the people of Tripoli that you tell me."

The old man remained quiet. Antonius sighed and turned to leave. But the old man pulled on his tunic as he stepped away. He held up two fingers.

"You saw two Persians...."

The old man nodded.

"Men?"

He nodded again and gestured that one was tall and one was short.

"A man and a boy. What did the man look like?"

The old man gestured in a cutting motion and pointed to his cheek, his neck, and his hands.

Narseh! Antonius said to himself. "He had scars. He was tall, dark skin, and thin with dark eyes?"

The old man nodded.

Antonius took him by the shoulders and looked directly into his eyes. "Which way did he go?"

The old man pointed down the road that headed southward along the coast.

"Thank you, my friend."

Antonius produced a small cloth, tied and filled with coins, and handed it to the old man, who weighed it back and forth between his hands before tucking it away, out of sight. The old man clasped his calloused hands in a grateful gesture and nodded. Antonius hurried back to his men.

* * *

The ship had been underway for days now. Just how many was difficult to discern. Asana's captors had given her bread and water to consume but had otherwise left her confined to this dank cage in the hold of the ship. It was a peculiar limbo, each moment the same as the last. Stale, salty air was the only air to breathe, and the creaking of the ship's bones as it bobbed and cut through the sea was the only sound to hear.

Eventually, the short man returned, this time wearing fine linen clothes and a turban instead of the rags he had worn when Asana so naively stopped to assist him.

He stood in front of the cage for a moment before saying, "I am Opilio. What is your name, girl?"

Asana spat at him.

"You dog! I was almost starting to have sympathy for you. You will learn to behave, as you belong to me now. And you will learn quickly! In a few days, we will dock in Alexandria, and we will see how valuable you are!"

He turned and left, saying nothing more.

Asana's heart dropped into her stomach. *I should have died in Antioch in the fires… or offered myself as a meal to the lioness that killed Bahram… or lived with Maren alone in Berytus,* she thought.

*   *   *

Many more miles passed under the hooves of their horses, but Antonius seemed no closer to finding the Persians he sought. His men were loyal and honor-bound to follow him, but even still, he could sense that their patience was wearing thin. He could scarcely blame them. They were men of action. For these Roman cavalrymen, travelling was simply a way to reach the battleground. And so far on this journey, there had been much travelling and no battlegrounds.

They reached the ruins of Berytus during the heat of the day, and they slowed the horses to a walk. The city had the feel of a mausoleum, and it did not seem right to rush through it at a gallop.

"God's wrath was surely spilled upon this city," one of the men said quietly.

They gazed upon the dusty stone foundations and crumbling walls as they made their way through the remnants of the city's roads. Antonius caught movement in the distance.

The man pointed and said, "There, sir."

"I saw it as well. A beast?"

They picked up their pace slightly and made their way closer. As they approached, a short figure ambled out from behind a stone wall. It was an old woman leaning heavily on her walking staff.

Antonius called out, "Hello! Old woman!" The figure looked up briefly but seemed uninterested and undeterred by the presence of a Roman cavalry vanguard. The men came directly up to her and put themselves in her path, and she looked up, seeming puzzled. "Old woman, we are seeking a few Persians who passed through Berytus recently."

The old woman responded in Aramaic, which Antonius could not understand. One of his men, however, was raised in Edessa and spoke the language well. He asked the question of the old woman in her language, and she responded softly in kind.

"She says there were three Persians who passed through here since the last new moon."

"Three? Ask her to describe them."

"She says yes, an older man, a younger man, and a girl."

"All together?"

The old woman shook her head and muttered to the soldier from Edessa.

"The girl came by first, the two men a day or two later."

"The man was tall and thin, with a scar across his cheek and neck…" Antonius gestured. "This is true, old woman?" She nodded. "And they went south?" he asked, pointing.

She nodded again. Antonius looked at his men and gave the signal to head southward before turning back to thank the old woman.

To Antonius' surprise, the old woman grabbed him by the wrist and stared straight into his eyes when he turned to her. The words she spoke he did not understand, but her meaning, a warning, was oddly clear to him.

"Sir?" said the soldier from Edessa cautiously.

"What did she say?"

"She… she said, 'Vengeance is written plainly on your heart, and so it is written on your future.'"

Antonius stood, taken aback. "What is this nonsense, old woman?"

Her gaze was transfixed on Antonius, and he could not deny the strange feeling in his gut. Her aged face seemed like only a mask that concealed a great power or secret. A secret that seemed to shine forth from her eyes like moonlight.

She spoke a long sentence as Antonius wondered at the woman. "Sir?"

"Yes…"

"She said, 'You have looked upon your true love and not known her once. So you shall do so a second time, still not knowing. And fate is cruel. For when you finally see, it will be through bittersweet eyes, for the end will not be far off!'"

Antonius pulled his wrist away from the old woman. After a prolonged silence, one of the men began to laugh. Soon, all the men were laughing riotously. Antonius smiled and forced a quick laugh. The cavalrymen set off in good spirits. But Antonius looked over his shoulder one last time, and the old woman stood motionless, staring back as they departed.

*   *   *

The ship had come to a halt some hours before, and there was some commotion on the deck above and the sound of many footsteps. Asana was filled with gnawing dread. A group of half a dozen men dressed in servant's clothes came below decks, with Opilio following behind.

"Men, those twelve casks there are to be brought back to your master at once. Tell him Opilio Lascarius appreciates the welcome he receives when he is in Alexandria. Tell him also that I have prepared a special gift that I shall deliver to him this evening after dinner. A little *Persian Delight*, you could say…"

"Yes, sir," one of the servants replied.

Opilio turned to Asana, and the two stared coldly at each other. He placed a bucket of water and a sponge just outside the iron cage. Reaching into his silken shirt, he produced a small bundle. He passed it through the bars.

"You will wash up, and then you will dress and prepare yourself for dinner," he said matter-of-factly.

"And if I say no?" Asana asked.

"Then there will be no dinner. Not tonight, not tomorrow night, and not the night after that."

"That is perfectly fine, as I would rather starve to death than accompany you to a dinner."

Opilio, bringing his hands to his heart and with a false frown, replied, "Oh! I am hurt, my dear! I offer you a chance to eat a luxurious meal in wealthy company, and you swat me away! Very well, I suppose I will have to arrive at dinner empty-handed. In the meantime, I wouldn't want you to be lonely. Perhaps these servants could keep you company?"

Opilio gestured toward the men who were handling the casks. They looked up to behold the girl in the cage, cracking vile grins and chuckling while they stared. Asana shuddered but maintained a stony appearance. Opilio turned after a moment and began to make his way back up to the deck of the ship.

"Wait..." Asana yelped. Opilio grinned and turned, relishing her change of heart. "I will accompany you..."

"Wonderful! I knew you would come around. We will leave in one hour."

Opilio climbed the ladder and disappeared above. Asana waited until he was out of sight to unwrap the bundle. Inside was a very immodest silk dress and a small glass bottle of perfume. She looked up at the servants who were watching her. They burst out laughing and joked amongst themselves in a language Asana could not understand. She could only imagine what was said. As the servants left with the casks, she had never felt more relieved to be alone...

*   *   *

They arrived in Tyre early in the morning after decamping from just north of the city. The men marveled at the gigantic stone causeway that connected the island to the shore. It had been built by Alexander the Great's army during a siege of the city nearly a thousand years earlier. Antonius, like all the Romans, had heard the tales of Alexander in his youth. But seeing the stone pier before them for the first time humbled all the men into silence. They approached the city, imagining the flaming arrows, javelins, and stones that the Tyrians would have rained upon them had they been the engineers in the great general's army all those centuries ago.

The alabaster walls of the city were as blinding as the sun itself. The men hitched their horses outside the gates and entered the city on foot. They were more cautious as they meandered through the city. This far beyond the Roman advance, it was impossible to know how many Persian men-at-arms might be present. The Romans walked the streets and alleyways, but in a city as busy as Tyre, finding just two people was going to be difficult.

By midday, the men had stopped at a tavern near the center of the city to purchase food and drink and to rest. They sat at a table, and the men joked and laughed as they ate. But Antonius was distant. He stared vacantly through the window and into the street. The people of Tyre were passing by, milling about with their goods and their animals, going about their business, not unlike the bustling streets of Constantinople. Yet he was so many miles from the capital of the empire. How had he ended up here?

He began reliving his journey: hearing the Patriarch Sergius on Easter morning bless the soldiers, setting out from Constantinople with Emperor Heraclius, scouting the hills around Tarsus and being ambushed, being imprisoned in that pit in Antioch... The memories were still so vivid. Then, as if on cue, a tall, thin man passed by outside. He was dressed as a Persian might dress, and on his face was a scar...

"Narseh!" Antonius whispered to himself.

He exploded out of his seat, stumbling and nearly knocking one of his men down in the process. The men were stunned, their eating and tale-telling interrupted by Antonius' sudden outburst. Once they had composed themselves, they dutifully followed their commander into the dusty avenue.

Antonius had become a hunting animal. His focus was absolute. He did not run but walked some distance behind his quarry. It had been a long journey to reach this point. He would not err as he had in Tarsus. He followed Narseh through the city until the Persian had turned into a stable near the city walls. *Perfect.* The faithful Romans followed their commander as he entered.

Once inside, Antonius watched as Narseh brought hay to his horse in one of the stalls.

Antonius gave fair warning. "Narseh!"

The Persian was clearly startled, but this gave way to confusion as he recognized the man speaking.

"Antonius Andronicus. You look well..." Narseh paused before adding, "I must admit, I am surprised that you lived."

"I feel more alive than ever at the moment."

"You brought so many men. Am I that fearsome a warrior?"

"They are only here as witnesses," Antonius replied tersely as he drew his sword.

"You have me at a disadvantage. I am afraid I am unarmed."

Antonius nodded to the soldier nearest him, who drew his sword and tossed it on the ground at Narseh's feet. Narseh bent and picked up the blade, saying, "Hm…honorable."

With little delay, the contest began. The first clang of metal striking metal spooked the horses throughout the stable. The gathered soldiers looked on silently. The melee was over quickly. Roman training was some of the greatest the world had ever known, and Antonius himself stood out even amongst his Roman peers. There was no hope for Narseh. With a final parry, the Persian was disarmed and forced down on one knee. The sword clattered off to the side, and Antonius grinned as he held the point of his blade to Narseh's throat.

Catching his breath, Narseh looked up and said, "Well, go on. Be done with it."

"Be done with it?" Antonius scowled. "You are lucky, Persian. If I had enough time, I would drag you back to Antioch behind my horse, starve you in that pit, and whip the flesh from your back." Narseh had no response. "Nothing left to say? Perhaps you would like to tell me where that swine, Ardashir, is hiding?"

"I would not tell you even if I knew, but the truth is that I do not know."

"I believe you. I believe you do not know. Though I am sure I could persuade you to speak, perhaps using some of your own methods!" Narseh stared silently, his mind seemingly distant. "Very well," Antonius said, "but just know that Ardashir will soon kneel as you kneel now, and this same blade will end his life."

Narseh remained silent. Antonius moved to Narseh's side and raised his sword. In a flash, Narseh lay dead at Antonius' feet.

But unbeknownst to the men in the stable, they were not the only witnesses to the death of Narseh. Hiding in a hay pile, peering out in unblinking horror, was a boy. His dark brown eyes were transfixed by the Roman raising the sword above his father's neck. Time slowed to a crawl for the boy. His mind took in every detail of the blade. The glints of light moved in concert with the sword itself as it began its descent. The sound of the blade hitting flesh and bone, the look of joy wrapped in anger on the Roman's face... and finally, the dull thud as the body and head of what was once his father slumped to the ground. The blood silently pooled on the hard dirt of the stable floor. The boy stared on. The Roman had an air of victory about him, and he spat on the lifeless body at his feet. The other Romans with him laughed.

How could one man do this to another? If the world was so full of hatred like this, what chance did the boy have? There could be no reconciliation with this Roman. There could be no peace. This man was evil and needed to face justice, and justice was the edge of a sword. As the boy watched these men laughing at his father's lifeless body, he felt a coldness enter and enwrap his heart. He was not conscious of it at first, but the specter soon enveloped him. His horror and despair had been usurped by a hardened calmness, a feeling the boy had never known before. Laying there in the hay, his eyes narrowed, and his breathing slowed. He studied every feature of the Roman's tanned face: his nose, his jaw, his eyes, even his ears. No, he would not forget this face. In his mind, the boy conjured scene after scene of the Roman's grizzly death at his hand.

The Romans pilfered what little they wanted from the body and then left the stable just as quickly as they had arrived. After a long time, the boy worked up the nerve and emerged from his hiding place in the hay. He stood over his father and beheld the grisly scene. Yes, he felt grief, but he was not feeling sadness. His feelings were more like clarity and eagerness. He knelt over his father's body and removed a leather cord from around the neck. Knotted up in the now blood-stained cord was a jackal's tooth. His father had worn it for as long as the boy could remember. The boy placed the jackal's tooth around his own neck and calmly, purposefully made his way out of the stable into the city.

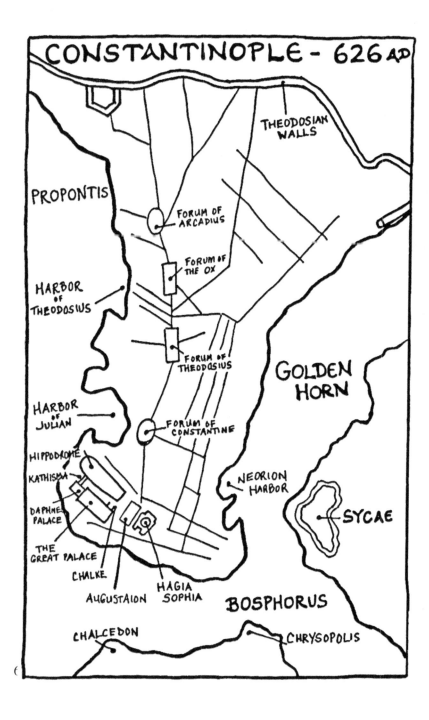

CONSTANTINOPLE - 626 AD

THEODOSIAN WALLS

PROPONTIS

FORUM OF ARCADIUS

FORUM OF THE OX

HARBOR OF THEODOSIUS

FORUM OF THEODOSIUS

GOLDEN HORN

HARBOR OF JULIAN

FORUM OF CONSTANTINE

HIPPODROME

KATHISMA

NEORION HARBOR

SYCAE

DAPHNE PALACE

THE GREAT PALACE

CHALKE

AUGUSTAION

HAGIA SOPHIA

BOSPHORUS

CHALCEDON

CHRYSOPOLIS

Chapter IV
Four Years Later
(May of 626 A.D.)

    Antonius stood atop the stone tower next to the Harbor of Theodosius in Byzantium. The tower was part of a seawall that surrounded the city on three sides. The fourth side, to the west, was first enclosed by the Walls of Constantine. The walls were large and had protected the city for almost a century. Emperor Theodosius had constructed even larger walls to enclose the parts of the city that had sprung up outside the Walls of Constantine. They were badly damaged by several earthquakes soon after and rebuilt each time by the citizens and soldiers of the city. Antonius never ceased to marvel at the Theodosian walls and the herculean effort taken to build and rebuild them. They were truly massive: forty feet tall, terraced, with nearly one hundred towers, gleaming alabaster visible from a great distance. The parapet wall was serrated and colored terracotta and must have looked like lion's teeth to all the invaders who had failed to overtake the city.

So imposing were the walls that many invading armies simply turned around rather than attempt the impossible feat of breaching the barrier. From his vantage point near the harbor, Antonius could see the Theodosian towers in the distance, standing vigilant against the enemies of the empire. He looked east out over the Bosphorus at Chalcedon in Asia Minor. The view was beautiful, and the cool spring air was invigorating. As calm as the moment was, there was a nagging wanderlust pulling at Antonius' feet.

Being stationed as a garrison commander in Byzantium was certainly a great honor, especially since it was bestowed upon Antonius by Emperor Heraclius himself! But the war—and the regaining of his honor—were not here. They were out beyond the Taurus mountains in Syria and Persia, because somewhere out there was Ardashir, the man who killed Urbicus. This was the same man who had starved and tortured Antonius and Francio, and for these offenses Antonius would take his revenge. He felt the anger welling up inside him.

At least now the Emperor was finally bringing the war to the Persian heartland near Ctesiphon after a desperate decade spent by the Romans on the edge of total collapse. A collapse that was halted only by the very walls on which he now stood. He often walked the seawalls around the city because it was his duty to keep track of the sentries and make sure none of the men slept during their watch. But he also truly enjoyed the walk itself. It gave him time to think and clear his head in the open air. His administrative duties often prevented him from taking these walks, and since Heraclius had promoted him to *tourmarch*, his administrative duties had expanded considerably.

Antonius looked on some other officers of his rank with distaste. Many had been promoted to their current positions by powerful family members or were born into an aristocratic lineage. Antonius considered himself apart from those officers of noble descent. He had earned his rank. They had not. They preferred to spend their time in the palaces and forums while their men performed their assigned duties in the field, but Antonius was very much a barracks officer. He preferred to spend time amongst his men, engaged in the same tasks they performed. On the battlefield, this attitude had earned him the loyalty of the men under his command. Here in Constantinople, it earned only the skepticism of both his subordinates and his superiors.

Because of this, Antonius often felt as alone in the middle of the bustling capital of the Roman Empire as he had at the bottom of the pit back in Antioch. The irony was not lost on him. The loneliness was only compounded by the monotony of his duties as garrison commander. It was a constant weight on his mind. To break the monotony, Antonius took to wearing the clothes of the ordinary citizens of Byzantium and walking through the city in the evenings. He would take a different route each time, stopping in taverns and walking down alleyways, visiting all the cisterns and chapels, and sitting by the docks in the harbors. He was certain that he had seen more of Byzantium than any other officer in the Roman army.

That evening, as Antonius stood atop the tower at the Harbor of Theodosius, he gazed off into the Propontis. The crescent moon hung low in the sky like a scythe, its dim light rippling off the surface of the water. There were several ships anchored in the harbor. Antonius was still staring toward the water as another ship approached, slowly entering the harbor. The men on the deck threw ropes to the dockworkers as the vessel drew near. A few moments later, the ship was moored at the wharf.

Antonius studied the ship. It appeared to be a Roman-style *corbita* with a single mast. He had seen hundreds like it, but this particular ship had ornate carvings on the prow, and the bowsprit looked as if it were plated with gold.

It must belong to a wealthy merchant or a foreign official, Antonius mused.

The dockworkers put up the plank, and three men disembarked.

The first man was bearded, portly, and dressed in fine clothing. Antonius guessed he was a Cappadocian from the way he had wrapped his head in cloth. The second man following behind him was massive. He stood head-and-shoulders above the first man, and in each hand, he effortlessly carried a large amphora. Lastly, there was a tall, thin man dressed in dark clothing with a curious, slow gait.

The three men were met at the end of the wharf by two Roman soldiers. This caught Antonius' full attention. He was too distant to hear what was said, but they smiled and laughed with each other. After what seemed like pleasantries, the portly man reached into his tunic and pulled out a coin purse. He handed each of the soldiers a coin and then motioned to the giant behind him, who handed off the amphora. The Romans turned and left, and the thin man followed in the same direction a few moments later. The short man and the giant boarded the ship again.

I will find those soldiers tomorrow and give them one chance to explain themselves, Antonius thought to himself.

In the meantime, he sat and waited, curious about this strange ship and the wealthy Cappadocian who arrived on it.

He didn't have to wait long before the two reappeared and disembarked again. This time, however, there was a third figure with them. The figure wore a hooded cloak, and the giant held them by the upper arm and rushed them down the wharf and into the city. One of the dockworkers removed the plank from the *corbita*, and the short Cappadocian handed the dockworker a coin before following the giant.

Antonius didn't waste any time and began following the Cappadocian toward the Forum of Arcadius. He kept his distance. He made sure not to catch his foot and give himself away as he navigated the dark streets. When he reached the forum, the Cappadocian paused and surveyed his surroundings before heading off the street into a tavern. Antonius had passed through this tavern before, and it was not the kind of place where respectable citizens could be found in the evenings. He quietly entered, laid a few bronze *nummi* on the bar, and asked for mead. The tavernkeeper produced a clay cup, and Antonius took it to a bench in the corner and sat.

He looked around casually. Almost every seat was full, and the sounds of raucous laughter and conversation drowned out all other noise. The tavern's denizens sat and drank amongst flickering lamps that cast twisted, wavering shadows on the brick walls. But even in the dim lamplight, there was no mistaking the giant across the room. And next to the giant sat the cloaked figure, barely visible and motionless. The Cappadocian was seated at a different table, speaking with a few others and laughing.

Antonius watched and waited, still unsure of what to make of it all. Soon, one of the men at the table placed something in the Cappadocian's hand. The Cappadocian turned toward the giant and nodded. The three men at the table stood up and walked over to where the giant was sitting. The men took the cloaked figure by the arm and walked out of sight toward the back of the tavern. Antonius stood and left the way he had entered. He stepped back onto the street and walked along the side of the building until he reached the dark alleyway behind. He paused and peered cautiously around the corner in time to see the three men and the cloaked figure emerge out of a wooden door at the rear of the building.

Rather than leave down the alleyway as Antonius assumed they would, the men pushed the figure down onto the dirt. The cloak was torn off, and the woman underneath gave a shout and kicked out at one of the men, startling him.

She was slapped and pinned down by another one of the men, and Antonius heard the man who she had struck say in Greek, "You are going to regret that, princess."

All three men were oblivious and inebriated. Now would be the time to act, but Antonius was an officer of the Roman legions. There would be consequences if a *tourmarch* was found to be at this tavern for any reason other than to quell a riot or make an arrest. Nevertheless, he chose to act.

He picked up a heavy stone and walked up behind the men unseen. Clasping the stone in one hand, he brought it down hard on the ribs of the man who was pinning one of the woman's arms down. The crack of bone and his immediate shout alarmed the others. By the time the second man looked up, Antonius' fist struck his face. The third man stumbled as he tried to stand but managed to grab Antonius around the waist. They grappled for a moment before Antonius threw him. The man rose to his feet again, and with a shout, he charged, but Antonius struck him down.

The back door swung open with a bang, and there stood the giant and the Cappadocian, taking stock of the situation. After looking at the three men groaning on the ground, the giant looked at Antonius and growled.

He took a step toward Antonius, but the Cappadocian barked, "Thrax, wait!" The short, paunchy Cappadocian stroked the graying beard that clung to his plump face and looked Antonius in the eyes for a few moments before motioning to the three men lying in the dirt. "Tell me, what did these men do to you that you have left them in such a condition?"

"They did nothing to me at all," Antonius replied.

The Cappadocian sighed. "Well, then, I am afraid you owe these gentlemen an apology as well as compensation."

Antonius scoffed. "And why would I do that?"

"Because they have paid for the use of this girl. She is my property."

"Your property? I am not so certain. Perhaps she is stolen… Perhaps that is why you needed to pay the guards at the harbor to go for a walk…."

The Cappadocian cocked his head, pausing briefly before retorting, "Hmph. No, not stolen. Rightfully acquired some years ago, in fact. And as for the guards, I was simply showing my appreciation for the Emperor's most underappreciated men."

Antonius laughed. "Well then, since she is your property, perhaps the *kommerkiarioi* can record your slave girl here and give you the Emperor's seal."

He pointed to the woman on the ground, who had backed up against the wall and covered herself with the cloak.

The Cappadocian turned dour. "If you are intent on ruining my business further by inviting a bickering *kommerkiarioi* into the matter, then I suppose I should just have Thrax here crush your skull."

At this, the giant smiled. The smile revealed yellowing, sharp teeth. The giant stared at Antonius with beady gray eyes that were set in a massive, bald head. He was made of muscle and stood nearly a foot above his Roman prey.

Antonius shook his head and smiled right back at the giant. "I am not sure that killing a Roman officer would be your wisest business decision. It might call attention to your other activities."

The Cappadocian looked Antonius up and down and said, "Although I do not believe you are an officer, it would seem to me that your physical abilities…." He paused, motioning to the three bodies on the ground. "Would suggest that you are indeed a soldier." He rubbed his palms for a moment then threw his hands up, saying, "So! It appears we are at an impasse. If I kill you, I risk my business, as you said. But if I don't kill you, I still risk my business since you could just as easily alert the *kommerkiarioi*."

Antonius nodded in agreement. He would have simply left the alley altogether, but his conscience would not allow him to leave the woman in the hands of this slimy merchant. To complicate matters further, Antonius was not sure he could grapple with the mountainous Thrax and come out alive.

He thought quickly. "Perhaps I could then suggest a compromise."

"Go on," the Cappadocian said, crossing his arms.

"Let us leave these three men be, and I will purchase your slave from you."

Thrax and the Cappadocian laughed heartily. "Not in a hundred years of soldiering could you afford this slave. She is the most beautiful Persian within a hundred miles and…" Antonius produced from his tunic several gold *solidi* and held them between his fingers for the Cappadocian to see. "*Solidi!*" There was a pause while his mind caught up to his eyes. "I believe… I believe we have an accord. Yes. The girl is yours. My name is Opilio Lascarius of…"

"Cappadocia," Antonius interjected as he handed Opilio the *solidi.*

"Why yes, that's right. And I bring all manner of goods from Asia, Syria, Judea, Aegyptus, and Cyrenaica, if you are in the market for…"

Antonius, ignoring the introduction, hurried over to the girl and pulled her up from the ground. He wrapped her cloak around her and headed down the alleyway, unsure exactly what his destination was. Thrax scowled at him as he walked past.

* * *

Asana was unsure how to take this turn of events. On the one hand, the immediate danger had passed. She had narrowly avoided the lascivious predations of the drunken men, and she was free of the vile Opilio. On the other hand, she was now at the mercy of a strange man in a strange land. Her hope was for a chance to escape, though she didn't have much of a plan from there. If she did escape, she would soon be recognized as a Persian, captured, and sold into slavery again.

She had become hardened to the world. For years, her entire life had been dictated by that disgusting Cappadocian and his brute. When she awoke each morning, chained to the planks in the dark hold of a ship, her only ambition was to survive the day. And she *had* survived. Day after endless day. But now she was being hurried through the alleyways of Byzantium, her fate again cast to the winds. Where was she being taken?

The walk was long, and Asana was already exhausted and starving. Her most recent meal, if it could be called a meal, had been the previous night on Opilio's ship. She was stumbling.

I wouldn't even have the strength to run if I had the chance, she thought to herself.

Asana's weariness and hunger were quickly overtaking her. Soon, her vision grew blurry, and she fainted.

* * *

Dammit, he thought. *How am I going to carry her the rest of the way?* Antonius considered the risk he was taking. A *tourmarch* who is charged with defending the capital of the Roman empire sneaking a slave girl—a *Persian* slave girl no less—onto the grounds of the imperial palace? If he were caught, he would face a lashing more severe than he had endured in Antioch. Even though the prudent decision would be to abandon the girl, his conscience again constrained his selfish instincts.

He threw the girl over his shoulder and walked back into the Forum of Arcadius.

Looking around, he thought frantically, *I am more than a mile from the palace. I need... I need a horse or a...*

Out of the corner of his eye, Antonius spotted a haycart against the side of one of the buildings in the forum. He made sure he was unseen and walked quietly to it, laying the girl's limp body in the cart. He curled her and made sure her whole body was obscured by her cloak. He grabbed hold of the haycart's handles and proceeded to slowly pull the cart from beside the building and head south back toward the harbor.

He was more than a mile from the palace, but he decided to take the longer route along the sea, avoiding the forums where possible. The old wooden wheels of the cart were far from silent, and he was sure he was going to attract attention on the way. Antonius plodded on diligently with his head down, but it wasn't long before he was proven right. While making his way along the coast road between the Harbor of Theodosius and the Harbor of Julian, a pair of soldiers walking atop the seawall took notice of him.

One of the soldiers looked down from the wall and shouted, "Who goes there?"

Your commanding officer, Antonius thought to himself. Instead, he replied, "Nobody of importance, sir."

"What is your business this late in the evening?"

At least my soldiers are doing their duty... "I am bringing this cart to the Hippodrome. I am told they are buying carts in preparation for the games on Sunday."

"Nobody is going to be buying anything at this hour. What do you have there?" the soldiers asked, gesturing at the cart.

"Just my cloak, sir. I intend to do my penance in the *Hagia Sophia* until sunrise. Then I will go to the Hippodrome." Antonius knew that most of his soldiers in the garrison were deeply religious men, and he was betting that these soldiers had likely gone to the *Hagia Sophia* more than once to repent for their own misdeeds.

The soldiers looming above Antonius on the wall had paused and exchanged glances. After sighing, the soldier said in a calmer, quieter voice, "Well, then go with the Lord, and may he light your way."

"God bless you both." Antonius had reservations about misusing the guards' convictions, but he reasoned that it was for the act of mercy he was now carrying out on behalf of the slave girl he had purchased.

The Patriarch Sergius' words came back to his mind, from all those years ago, before setting out on a campaign with Emperor Heraclius, *"Mercy is most transformative... when it is bestowed by one sinner on another...."*

He continued on with the haycart, the girl not stirring once. As the archways and the pillars of the Hippodrome came into view in the moonlight, Antonius was forced to confront the problem at hand: *What was he going to do with this girl?*

His conscience had ruled out abandoning the girl, even though that was the course of action with the least risk to him. He had no family in the city and no friend he trusted enough to leave the girl with. Francio could be trusted, but he was hundreds of miles away, fighting the Persians on the way to Ctesiphon with Emperor Heraclius. That left Antonius with only one option: he would have to bring the girl to his personal quarters.

His quarters were in the Palace of Daphne. The Palace of Daphne was but one wing of the Great Palace that was designed three centuries before. Emperor Constantine had erected it while he was transforming Byzantium from a small Greek village into Constantinople, the grandest city in the world. The Great Palace itself was a sprawling complex with hundreds of chambers and halls linked by endless runs of ornate passageways, terraces, and walls. Marble statues of emperors and generals were found everywhere, and the most detailed mosaics covered floors and walls. The palace was pure splendor.

But to reach his quarters in the Palace of Daphne, Antonius would have to pass through the *Chalke* gate. The towering bronze gate served as the only passable entrance into the Great Palace. And at this hour, the gate would certainly be closed. Were he by himself, Antonius would simply tell the palace *excubitors* to open the gate for him. They were under his command after all. But to bring a commoner, a Persian commoner no less, into the Great Palace would arouse suspicions.

Antonius had reached the southern end of the palace complex, and he paused there to think through his dilemma. Time passed, and he could think of nothing. He dropped his shoulders and threw his head back, defeated. He noticed that the dimness of the crescent moon allowed all the stars to shine brilliantly. When he was a *pentarch* in the vanguards, he would have plenty of time to gaze upon the celestial spheres while the men were encamped for the night. Sleeping in the open afforded that one, not-so-insignificant luxury. But here in Byzantium, his eyes seldom had a chance to divert from his assigned duties.

As he looked up at the sky, a shooting star flickered to life, etched its small, blue track onto the face of the heavens, and disappeared as suddenly as it came. He stared at the spot in the sky where it vanished for some time, and when he lowered his gaze back towards the earth, his eyes came to rest on the hulking silhouette of the Hippodrome... and the *Kathisma*.

"The *Kathisma!*" Antonius said aloud, "of course!"

The Emperors and their guests had their own seating on the upper deck of the Hippodrome, called the Emperor's Lodge. This *Kathisma* was connected by a covered stone bridge to the Great Palace.

The gates on either side of the bridge were locked too, but it was Antonius who held the key. The key, however, was in his quarters. He stared at the bridge over the alley between the Hippodrome and the palace and sighed. There was only one way this was going to work. He would have to leave her in the Hippodrome, go through the *Chalke* gate, make it to the Palace of Daphne, unlock the doors to the *Kathisma*, and then retrieve the girl from the Hippodrome. *Simple,* he thought, lying to himself.

Antonius hauled the haycart through one of the stone archways into the Hippodrome and left it in a nook in the darkness. He quickly made his way back outside and down the causeway between the two great buildings. He moved briskly. It was unlikely that anyone would stumble upon the girl in the back of the cart, but he was taking no chances. Besides, he had plenty of ground to cover—a quarter mile to the Column of Justinian, another two hundred paces through the *Augustaion* to the *Chalke* gate, and then another quarter of a mile through the palace grounds to his quarters.

Antonius stopped and caught his breath as he approached the *Augustaion*. Fully composed, he turned the corner, and the familiar sight of the *Chalke* came into focus. The torches mounted on the archways cast the bronze lattice of the massive gate in a fearsome light. There could be no other way in the heart of the Empire! He approached the gate in his normal manner. And why not? He came through this gate several times a day. But the *excubitors* standing guard met him as he approached, and one placed his palm on Antonius' chest.

"No further," the guard said.

I am not in uniform… Antonius remembered. Crossing his arms, he spoke in an authoritative tone, "Soldier… is this how you greet your commanding officer?"

A flash of recognition crossed their faces, and they straightened up and saluted. "I am sorry, sir. It's… we did not recognize you, sir."

"What is your name?"

"Isaac, sir."

"And where do you come from?"

"Chrysopolis, sir."

"How long have you been in service to the Empire?"

"Six months, sir."

"Tonight, I wanted to make sure none of the men were asleep in the watchtowers. Dressed as *tourmarch*, they would have known of my approach. They say that as a man climbs in rank, his footsteps grow louder. Do you understand?"

"Yes, sir."

"Good. It's late, and I would like to get to my quarters."

"Yes, sir." Isaac stepped forward and turned to look up the wall. He put his hand to his mouth and shouted, "Gates up, half!"

Moments later, the iron chains rang out, and the *Chalke* slowly opened its mouth. Antonius slipped under as soon as he was able.

Now inside the walls of the Great Palace grounds, he marched straight toward the Daphne Palace. He walked down ornamented garden pathways past the senate hall, the barracks, and the reception hall. He ascended the grand marble staircase, which led to the second floor of the palace, and hurried down the hall to the heavy wooden doors at the entrance to his quarters. Antonius entered, grabbed the bronze key from beside the door, and continued down the hallway, following the turns until he reached the doorway that led to the *Kathisma*.

He unlocked the door and closed it behind him, then made his way across the bridge over the causeway and unlocked the door on the other side. From there, it was a mad dash down the steep staircases of the Hippodrome to the nook by the archway where he had left the cart. *But which archway was it?* Antonius somewhat frantically darted between the archways of the stadium, looking for the haycart. He was greatly relieved when he found it just as he had left it. He threw the girl over his shoulder once more and climbed the steep steps back up to the *Kathisma*. He was exhausted when he reached the top and crossed the bridge on shaking legs, breathing heavily. Safe inside the Daphne Palace, he locked the door to the *Kathisma* and made his way into his quarters.

He set the girl down on the bed. *This is foolish,* Antonius said to himself. *The Emperor is out campaigning against the Persians, and here I am, sneaking a Persian into the very heart of the empire!* He sat on the edge of the bed in his chamber and cursed himself. *Tomorrow I must make the rounds in preparation for the chariot races. I cannot be hidden away. But I also cannot leave the girl here on her own.*

After wrestling with his own thoughts for a time, Antonius resigned himself to the only solution he could think of. Heading out of the Palace of Daphne once more, he made the long walk to the armory. He grabbed an iron chain and fetter and quickly made his way back to his quarters. To his relief, she had still not awoken. In the corner of his quarters were several steps. These steps rose and curved toward a door that opened to the inside of a turret, from which he could look down on much of the palace grounds and the Hippodrome.

Antonius carried the girl up the steps into this tower room and laid her on the floor. He ran the chain through the iron loop in the stone wall and went to place the fetter around her ankle. He was stopped and taken aback by her appearance. The girl was so thin! Who knew how long she had been enslaved to that odious merchant? He brought food and water from his room and placed them beside her.

For the first time, Antonius had a moment to study the girl. She lay on the stone floor, her head resting on her arm. On her wrist was a wide copper bangle. Leather thongs were woven through the bangle, pinning a few sand-colored feathers in place. She had a spiraling copper armlet on her upper arm. The long, dark waves of her hair spilled onto the floor. Her face appeared troubled as she slept, but even still, her beauty was stunning. Her perfectly smooth skin, her plush lips like lily petals. Antonius sighed heavily as he got back to the task at hand. *I have no other option,* he told himself as he clasped her ankle in iron.

He left the tower and barred the door. Satisfied that he had done everything he could for the time being, he collapsed onto the bed and fell into a deep sleep.

* * *

Asana awoke with a terrible thirst. She tried to open her eyes but was blinded by the bright sunlight. *Where am I?* The last thing she could remember was that Roman soldier confronting Opilio. As her eyes adjusted to the light, she sat up and began rubbing her temples. She noticed a familiar heaviness, looked down at her ankle, and saw it fettered in iron.

"Of course," she said, defeated.

From one cruel master to another. Why even go on? It was a question she had asked herself many times in the hold of Opilio's ship. She had not come up with an answer but resolved to keep searching for one. For now…

In front of Asana was a wooden tray that she had only now become conscious of. The tray held a pitcher full of water and many fruits and nuts. She grabbed the pitcher and nearly finished its contents without stopping. The food did not last much longer. It was as good a meal as she had eaten in many years, except for the occasions when Opilio would bring her along to dine with his *friends*. With her hunger and thirst partially abated, she listened closely for any sign of the man who had brought her to this place. There was nothing to be heard but muffled, distant noises from the city that carried through the stone window on the breeze. An exasperated sigh welled up from her heart, and she sprawled back onto the floor in resignation.

Her mind played tricks on her as she began to drift. She felt the floor swaying as if on the sea again, only to sit up with a start when she realized she was not. Fevered memories rushed through her mind, images of faces and places she had known. They came unrelentingly, in no sensible order. Asana grew lightheaded and shivered. She laid back down, closing her eyes in search of relief, and found only the phantom sensation of waves moving the floor under her. Much time passed before she finally found sleep.

* * *

Antonius had awoken that morning in a rush. He had slept longer than he intended to, and he needed to make up for his lost time. Donning his *caliga* sandals, tunic, and belt, he quickly checked on the girl, who was still sleeping. He grabbed his sword and sheathed it in his belt, barred and locked the door to his quarters, and headed through the causeway to the *Kathisma* in the Hippodrome.

There, after meeting with his messengers and officers, he sent for Isaac, the young soldier guarding the *Chalke* gate the night before. Isaac arrived looking fairly concerned, as any soldier might be when summoned by their overall commander.

"Sir?"

"Isaac, right?"

"Yes, sir."

Antonius studied the soldier. He was muscular but thin, barely filling out his breastplate. His face was not quite a man's face, yet his taut mouth and brown eyes were focused enough to convey a maturity beyond his years. "Have you been on campaign yet?"

"No, sir. I volunteered to go east to Persia."

"Volunteered? Exceptional. But they stationed you in the city because of your age?"

"Yes, sir."

Antonius paused before deciding abruptly. "Today, I am promoting you to *topoteretes*. You will be my deputy and report directly to me. I will inform your commanding officer to find a replacement for your post."

Isaac looked somewhat shocked, "Yes, sir... thank you, sir."

"Your first assignment is to find the two men who were posted to the Harbor of Theodosius last night and bring them to me."

"Yes, sir!" Isaac dutifully set off at once, striding much more energetically than he had on his way in.

Antonius continued about his business for the day, fending off the exhaustion that had followed him from the night before. Tomorrow, the colossal Hippodrome would be brimming with the citizens of the capital, all frenzied and cheering for their favorite charioteers. Wine would be flowing in abundance, and the chariot races had a long history of rapidly descending into chaos.

Despite the costly war, Emperor Heraclius had expressly ordered that the races and games continue while he campaigned against the Persians. But with most of the army hundreds of miles to the east, the capital was undermanned. Thus it fell to Antonius to ensure that the Emperor didn't have to send any men back to assist if a riot broke out. This was no small feat.

Some hours later, while Antonius was conducting a final review of the preparations for the races, Isaac returned with two soldiers in tow.

"Sir!" Isaac said forcefully as he saluted.

"These are the two men?" Antonius asked.

"Yes, sir."

"Thank you, Isaac," Antonius said, dismissing his newly promoted deputy. "Comrades, am I correct to say that you were stationed at the Harbor of Theodosius last night?"

"Yes, sir," they answered in unison.

"Did anything unusual happen during your watch?"

"No, sir," again in unison.

"Really? There were no Cappadocian merchants bribing the soldiers on watch and smuggling in captives?" Antonius asked, staring directly into the men's eyes.

The question had the desired effect. The color drained from their faces. They had been found out, and they both knew there was no escape from guilt.

"In days past, soldiers taking bribes would be imprisoned, whipped, and expelled from service, living out the remainder of their lives in dishonor. It is only right! How can the Empire function if the Empire's soldiers are loyal to the highest bidder rather than loyal to their fellow citizens and the Emperor himself? Isaac, the young man who brought you to me, and others are *honored* to serve the Emperor and would do so even without pay! And here you are, forsaking your duties for a merchant's table scraps!"

The men remained silent, awaiting the *tourmarch* Antonius' judgment. "Do you have wives? Children?"

"Yes, sir."

Antonius sighed heavily, letting the silence afterwards hang around the accused soldiers' necks. "I will allow you to remain in service to the Empire, but you will forfeit the month's pay. Further, the two of you will join the servants who muck the stables during the races. Any additional instance of dishonoring the Empire will lead you to prison. Am I understood?"

"Yes, sir!"

The men looked extremely relieved. They had expected a flogging at the very least. But in truth, Antonius could not spare the time to incapacitate or expel any of the men. The situation was too delicate, the army too undermanned, and the war effort too important.

"Report to the stables immediately. You are dismissed." The two pardoned men saluted and began to depart in haste. "Hold on a moment." They stopped and turned back to

82

attention. "There was the merchant, his giant, and his captive. But there was a fourth as well. Who is he?"

"Sir?" one of the men asked.

"There was a tall, thin man with the merchant. Who is he?" Antonius pressed.

"He… the merchant, has a young Persian he travels with," the soldier answered.

"A servant?"

"Perhaps a deckhand, sir."

"Hm… that is all."

The men headed off toward the stables, leaving Antonius with few answers and more questions. A Persian inside the city walls was a cause for concern. The thought only reminded Antonius of the Persian currently chained in his quarters. Antonius sighed heavily again and began to hurry, hoping to complete his duties and return to the palace as soon as possible.

* * *

Opilio removed his turban and ran his hand through his greasy hair. The *corbita* bobbed and swayed on its moorings in the harbor. The sail of his boat provided some meager shade from the midday heat. "Soroush!" he barked while fanning himself. The tall, thin young man came up from below decks. He had deeply tanned skin, dark brown eyes perched over sharp cheeks, and a prominent nose. His uncut black hair nearly covered his ears, and on his boyish face was a thin mustache. He climbed just high enough to see Opilio through the hatch in the deck. "See how much oil we have left. The innkeeper wanted to purchase as much as we could spare. You and Thrax can take the oil to him this evening."

"Fine," Soroush answered without moving.

"Well, go on then! What is the hold-up?" Opilio asked.

"Where is the girl?" Soroush asked. Opilio chuckled.

"Well... she won't be travelling with us any longer. Some Roman soldier purchased her last night. It saved his life. Thrax was going to crush his skull."

"A Roman soldier?" Soroush pressed.

"Yes. Said he was an officer, but he wasn't dressed as one. He certainly had enough money, though..."

"What did he look like?"

"What the hell does that matter!" Opilio shouted, "Get down there and count the oil casks."

Soroush obliged and trudged back down into the hold of the ship. He had been working for the Cappadocian merchant for a few years now. Opilio had been impressed with his seriousness and reliability when they met. At the time, he had told the young Soroush, "My friend Thrax here makes a great impression, but I need somebody who can move about unnoticed and *think* if the occasion calls for it." The young Soroush accepted the job, having nothing to lose.

It seemed that boarding Opilio's ship turned out to be a wise decision for the youthful Soroush. The former street rat now had a place to lay his head, food to eat, and coins in his pouch. In time, he grew fond of the sea voyages, which allowed him to see many parts of the world that had been unknown to him. Opilio, though ornery, had been generally fair to him and Thrax. The same fairness did not necessarily extend to Opilio's clients, though the presence of the giant Thrax tended to keep accusations of foul play to a minimum.

Soroush had told Opilio little about his upbringing, not that Opilio cared in the least one way or the other. The boy's work was consistent, and his stoic disposition gave the merchant little cause to wonder or worry. But behind Soroush's calm, dark eyes was a smoldering ember, a vendetta from long ago. Soroush was not distracted by it, even though it burned slowly and unceasingly in the back of his mind. Quite to the contrary, it kept him focused.

The ember was a constant in his life, waiting for the right moment to burst into flame. And Soroush was certain that moment would come, even if he must wait years. And when it did come, Soroush would have his vengeance. Only then would the ember die out. But for the moment, he would walk the hold of Opilio's ship and count the oil casks…

*   *   *

Asana lay against the cool stone, peering up at the night sky through the oriel windows of the tower. Her life, it seemed, was to be one misery after another. Happiness, like the stars above, was forever out of reach. She listened to the breeze rustling the leaves outside. The gentle sound was like a lullaby, and she used it to drift off, just like she had with the sound of the waves when she was trapped in the hold of that dreadful ship.

She had nearly fallen asleep when she heard the outer door open quietly and slow footsteps entering. *The barbarian has finally returned,* she thought to herself. The footsteps approached the steps to her chamber door. The door opened slowly, and there he was again. *What does he want?* He looked at her sitting down against the stone, looking back at him.

After a moment, he spoke, "I must go to the Hippodrome tomorrow with several of the other officers. I need to know that you will stay here and not try to leave."

Asana said nothing and stared coldly.

"Listen, I cannot keep you safe in this city. They will know you for a Persian, and you will be sold to another merchant, and they will likely have my head for harboring you." Again, Asana said nothing. Antonius inhaled, his exasperation getting the better of him. "Don't you understand what a risk I have taken? You won't even tell me if you understand me!" Asana continued staring for a moment and then looked away, indifferently gazing toward the sky. Antonius felt his blood beginning to boil, and he rushed up and grabbed her roughly by the shoulders and turned Asana so she faced him. "Answer me!"

Asana pushed as hard as she could to free herself, but it was like pushing against a stone pillar. She flailed, clawing at his chest, drawing blood, and tearing his tunic. He released her and pushed her down in frustration.

"Bah!" he grumbled as he waved his hand at her dismissively.

He made his way to the door. Just before he stepped out of the chamber, Asana caught a glimpse of something curious around his neck. A small glint of metal was revealed by the tear in his tunic: a ring... a silver ring with a single crescent jade...

Chapter V
The Castle in the Sky

Early the next day, the chattering birds could be heard through the palace windows. The morning sun was chasing off the cool dampness that had settled in overnight. Antonius had risen early. He brought the girl water and food and headed back towards the door without speaking.

As he was nearly through the doorway, she spoke, "The ring around your neck." Antonius was stunned into silence. First by hearing her voice for the first time, second by the fact that this Persian girl was fluent in Greek, and third by the unexpected topic of conversation. "The ring… how did you come to possess such a ring?"

Antonius laughed to himself and shook his head. "You keep silent for days, refusing to even say a word, and suddenly

I am supposed to start telling you stories? You have nerve, Persian. Enjoy your meal."

He stepped away but was interrupted again.

"Please… the ring. Tell me," she persisted, her voice taking on an earnest tone.

Antonius was persuaded, not necessarily by her, but by his own curiosity. *What is this ring to her?* he wondered.

He thought for a moment before he put his answer to her. "Many years ago, when I was in a very dark place, someone who was kind and merciful kept me alive and happened to give me this ring."

"Give?" Asana asked.

Antonius was puzzled. "I found it and never had the chance to return it or thank her."

"Who was this person?"

"I don't know," Antonius replied truthfully.

She pressed on. "You don't know?"

"I do not know. Now I think it is my turn for questions, yes? Why are you so concerned about this ring?"

"Because I had a ring that looked exactly the same."

Antonius now felt somewhat obliged to humor her. "Is that so? And what happened to your ring?"

"I lost it. It fell off my finger when I… when I was in a hurry."

"Oh?"

"Yes," she answered.

"And I suppose you expect me to believe that this is yours! Do you take me as a fool? How long ago? And where did you lose this ring?"

"Many years ago, in Antioch."

Antonius froze, and his mouth went dry. Swallowing around the lump in his throat, he said quietly, "Antioch…."

"Yes."

"Years ago, Antioch was not a very friendly place. What was a young girl doing in Antioch back then?"

"My father was an officer in the Persian army. He and I and my brother lived at the fortress with the other soldiers in the garrison."

A simple "Hmm" was all Antonius could manage. He pressed at his brow and slowly shook his head as his mind raced. "It is impossible," he muttered to himself, barely above a whisper.

"What is impossible?" Asana asked, tilting her head with curiosity.

"Do you remember the day you lost your ring?"

"Yes. The Romans were attacking, and my father sent my brother and me away on horseback. I left everything behind, including the ring. It was my mother's, whom I knew only in the womb."

Antonius nodded, though his mind was far away, falling back through his memories and landing in that forsaken pit in Antioch... *How could it be? I don't believe it...* A heavy rapping at the door to his quarters interrupted his thoughts.

"*Tourmarch* Andronicus! Your orders are needed, sir!"

Antonius approached Asana, gripped her shoulders, and spoke to her in a harsh whisper, "You must remain quiet. This is the only place I can keep you safe. You have to trust me! We are at war with Persia, and these men are soldiers. They would not be kind to you if they found you. I must go to the races today, but I will return tonight. You must remain quiet. Do you understand?"

Asana nodded tentatively, seeing no other choice before her.

The soldier's shout came again from the hallway outside Antonius' quarters, "*Tourmarch*?!"

Antonius secured the door to the tower room and hurried toward the entrance of his quarters. "Yes, comrade. I hear you." He opened the door, and two young soldiers stood hesitantly, staring. "Well? What is the matter? Have the Persians breached the walls?" he asked with feigned concern.

"No, sir, we… sir, we have a woman who insists that she is to be seated with the *tourmarch*…."

"And you need me to do what? Arrange battle formations?" Antonius laughed.

The two young soldiers looked at each other warily.

This time the other spoke, "Sir… she said that she was the wife of your dear friend, and there would be grave consequences for us if you were to find out we denied her entry into the Emperor's Lodge, where she wishes to view the races."

Eris. Antonius knew with certainty that there was only one woman bold enough to demand entry into the Emperor's Lodge: Eris, the dauntless wife of Francio. "Well, comrades, if she is the woman I think she is, then there would indeed be grave consequences for crossing her."

"Sir?"

"Tell her to take her seat. I will join her shortly."

"Yes, sir," the pair said in unison.

Antonius dressed and draped his red cape across his shoulders. Though he had planned the security of the races thoroughly and his men were armed and sober, he decided to bring his sword and don his breastplate anyway. Any competition between the *Blues* and *Greens* at the Hippodrome was never more than one careless insult away from spiraling into a brawl—or worse.

He exited his chamber and checked the lock on the door twice before making his way to the causeway and into the *Kathisma*.

Isaac approached him as he entered, saluted, and reported. "Sir, the men are all in position, and the crowds have begun to find their way to their seats. There are no incidents to report so far. The opening ceremony will begin in less than an hour."

"Thank you, Isaac. Please make the rounds to the stables and ensure that our two penitent soldiers from yesterday are taking no breaks."

"Yes, sir," Isaac replied enthusiastically, departing immediately.

Antonius took a deep breath and looked around him. The Hippodrome, like the palace and indeed the entire city, was a marvel to behold. No matter how often he made his way through the great stadium, the feeling of wonder and awe was never lost. The racing track below encircled a row of massive obelisks and columns, monuments to the great achievements of the empire and its emperors. The two teams of charioteers and horsemen, Green and Blue, would soon race around these monuments seven times. The hooves of the best horses in the empire would summon a dusty maelstrom, while the citizens of the capital would roar cries of glorious victory or bitter defeat from the stone tiers rising up from the track.

Near the center of the track on the upper tier was the covered colonnade of the Emperor's Lodge, the *Kathisma*. Connected directly to the palace by the elevated causeway, the emperors had for generations come to view the races from this luxurious vantage point. Indeed, it was one of the few times the ordinary citizens could see their Emperor, and it fostered a great sense of pride and unity amongst the people to be enjoying the same games as their sovereign... if the celebratory end of the races didn't devolve into rioting, of course.

Today, the Emperor was conspicuously absent. The empire had been on the brink of collapse until Heraclius ascended to the throne and took control of the armies in the field directly. There was anxiety among the people about the war, but their confidence in Emperor Heraclius' steady-handed leadership had grown over the years. Even still, the throne in the center of the Kathisma was visible from the entire amphitheater. Its ornate gold-leafed adornments and royal purple silk draped over the arms drew great attention to its emptiness.

"Antonius, there you are!"

Antonius immediately recognized the sweet, lilting voice. "Eris, it has been some time."

"Yes, you seem to be the busiest man in the Empire!" Eris' disarming smile did much to soften her assertive stance and piercing blue eyes. Her delicate nose and thin frame accentuated her femininity, but the weight of her presence and personality were undeniable.

"Well, the races do not plan themselves," Antonius offered dryly.

"I am teasing, darling. Try not to be so serious!" Eris straightened, holding her pointer finger in the air. "Oh! There is someone I want you to meet!" She turned and ushered a woman to Antonius. "This is Julia. Her husband served alongside you and my Francio."

Antonius watched as a woman, graceful in her movements, reached out to clasp his hands. She had dark hair and skin that was smooth like glass. Her expression was very reserved. Her lips pursed in a polite smile, but her doe eyes revealed little emotion at all.

She spoke quietly, saying, "Urbicus thought very highly of you."

Antonius was pained at the memory of his comrade, who had not survived his imprisonment in Antioch. "Urbicus was a great man. It is I who should speak highly of him."

Julia simply nodded in thanks and cast her eyes downward.

"Please, ladies, will you join me?" Antonius asked,

"Yes, certainly. I must say, your etiquette has greatly improved since you became an officer, Antonius," Eris taunted.

"That was never my intention, Eris. I assure you," Antonius replied, showing the women to their seats. He motioned to one of the servants stationed in the *Kathisma,* who quickly made his way to Antonius. "Three cups of wine."

"Yes, sir," came the reply.

They sat in three cushioned seats reserved for the *tourmarch* and his guests.

"How comfortable," Julia remarked, clearly unacquainted with palace luxury.

Soon after, the servant returned and handed out three wide silver cups. The dark wine had a delicious, warming aroma.

Antonius raised his cup to his guests and said, "To the safe return of noble Francio." Thinking for a moment, he added, "And to the memory of noble Urbicus." The women raised their glasses, though Antonius could see that the very mention of Urbicus' name hurt Julia. They drank and savored the taste. "Some of the best grapes in the empire," Antonius offered.

"Delicious," Eris concurred, drinking deeply again.

"This place is so beautiful..." Julia said, looking toward the center of the *Kathisma.*

There were ornately appointed marble columns supporting the roof. In front of the Emperor's seat, over the bronze railing, and down several steps were four bronze horses. The statues were life-size and exquisitely detailed. When viewed from elsewhere in the Hippodrome, it gave the appearance that the Emperor's throne was a chariot drawn by horses.

"The cost and the effort must have been tremendous," Julia continued.

"Millions of coins, thousands of men, and hundreds of years were consumed in the making of this place. Every time I come here, I am moved at the thought of it," Antonius said.

"I did not realize you were so sentimental...." Eris jibed. Julia smiled to herself, and Antonius simply sighed. "Oh, look! I think we are about to begin!" Eris exclaimed, pointing across to the gates on the arena floor, which were now rising.

Antonius, along with the rest of the crowd, grew quiet and stood as two men emerged from the gate.

The first was Sergius, the Patriarch of Constantinople. He was dressed in a white robe, with a pale *cpitruchellon* draped around his shoulders and a simple *kamelaukion* on his head. With both hands, he held a staff in front of him. Atop the staff was a simple wooden crucifix. Behind Sergius, at a respectful distance, walked another simply dressed man with his head bowed and hands clasped. Antonius recognized the man as Bonus, a well-liked patrician and the *strategos* of all the soldiers not currently on campaign with the Emperor.

The two men made their way to the center of the arena and stepped up onto the *Spina,* the central barrier that the charioteers would soon be racing around. They both looked about and beheld the tens of thousands who now looked back upon them. The graying patriarch and the stern patrician motioned for the people to be seated, and the people dutifully complied.

Antonius, Julia, and Eris watched and listened deferentially as the Patriarch Sergius and the Patrician Bonus invoked God's favor upon the people, the games, the Emperor, and the Empire. The whole of the Hippodrome watched in almost complete silence. The races in this place were a pillar of the city's culture, an escape from the toils of daily life, an escape from the war, which had dragged on longer than many in the audience had been alive.

The Patriarch proclaimed, "We have suffered, we have endured many hardships, we have overcome many obstacles. But we have retained God's favor through our faith in his deliverance of us from all our foes, famines, and plagues. For the walls around this great city, though they be stone, gain their strength only through God's will. Should he but remove his finger from the altar in the *Hagia Sophia*, all of the battlements and towers would rejoin the dust in an instant, and our enemies would triumph that very day. So, it is with great humility that we beseech the Lord's continued favor. We offer these games and celebrations to give thanks so that his people on Earth might enjoy a day of rest and happiness."

The Patriarch then led the crowd in prayer, and the entire amphitheater sounded the passage in one voice:

Our Father, who art in heaven,
Hallowed be thy name;
Thy kingdom come;
Thy will be done
on earth, as it is in heaven:
Give us this day our daily bread;
And forgive us our trespasses,
as we forgive them that trespass against us;
And lead us not into temptation,
But deliver us from evil;
For thine is the kingdom,
and the power, and the glory,
For ever and ever.
Amen.

It had been many years since there were games held in the Hippodrome. With the tremendous strain of the war effort, scarcely a horse could be spared for entertainment. But now, with the opening ceremonies and prayers complete, years of anxiety and monotony were giving way to a palpable excitement. The horses could be seen lining up at the starting gate, and a hush fell over the stadium.

Then the sudden blast of the trumpet came, and the first heat of charioteers scrambled off the starting line. The thunder of the iron-clad hooves was quickly drowned out by the thunder of the crowd, roaring, cheering, and cursing each time one chariot overtook another. By the time the first lap was complete, a great tail of dust had churned up and cast a haze over the whole spectacle.

"What a messy ordeal!" Eris shouted over the roar of the crowd.

"This is no mess," Antonius chided. "Just imagine if they were gladiators instead of charioteers!"

Julia, who had been somewhat reserved until now, smiled widely and applauded along with the crowd. The chariots entered their final lap. The audience had worked themselves into a frenzy. Their raucous shouts and cheers came to a head when the finish line was crossed. Trailing a blue flag, the victorious racer took an extra lap at a slower pace, saluting and waving to the crowd as he did so. The other charioteers made their way through the gates and off the track. The people in the stands either cheered or booed the winner during his victory lap, depending on whether their loyalties lay with or against the 'blue' charioteers.

"How many races will there be?" Julia asked, clearly excited now.

"Seven," came Antonius' answer. He noticed that Julia seemed pleased by this. "There will be other performances as well, see?"

He pointed toward the gates. A smallish man appeared, wearing pointed red cloth shoes with bells on the ends. He wore yellow pants, an oversized red tunic, and a yellow cap with a bell. The jester puffed out his chest and walked proudly, swinging his arms with a giant smile on his face. Suddenly he stopped, his smile turning into surprise, and pointed his finger in the air.

He reached down into his tunic and pulled out a stick with a wooden horse's head mounted on the end. Julia laughed along with most of the audience, and Eris rolled her eyes. Antonius smiled. With a determined look on his face, the jester promptly mounted the *horse* and set off around the track. Not having made it halfway around the track, his speed began to slow, and he began to act as though his horse was being stubborn. Laughter billowed from the crowd.

He fought futilely with his wooden steed and came to a full stop. After scratching his head for a moment, the jester pointed his finger in the air again. Reaching into his tunic, he pulled out another stick. This stick had a string tied to its end. Then, reaching into his shoe, the jester pulled out a carrot, displaying it to the audience, whose laughter had doubled. He tied the carrot to the string and cautiously held it in front of his horse, which promptly set off at full speed.

Now, bells jingling and hanging on for dear life, the jester tried frantically to grab the carrot that was bouncing back and forth, but to no avail. Next, he tried catching it in his mouth, eventually succeeding. His wooden horse reared to a halt to the delight of the crowd, who applauded and shouted, "Bravo, bravo!" But the jester put his finger to his lips and motioned furiously for the crowd to be silent, and they obliged.

He slowly and cautiously pulled the carrot out of his teeth and held it in his hands. He gripped it at either end and snapped it as quietly as he could, but his fake horse heard the noise and perked up, and the jester stood frozen in fear. When the horse settled down, the jester again snapped a piece of the carrot and tossed it a few steps ahead. The horse perked up and trotted over, the jester manipulating the stick to make it appear as if the horse bent to eat the treat.

The jester, smiling at his own genius, tossed the next piece of carrot slightly further, and the horse trotted out to eat again. Emboldened, the jester set up to throw the rest of the carrot, but as his arm moved through the air, he sneezed, and the carrot flew all the way to the end of the track. The horse's head turned to look at the jester, whose face was panic-stricken. The audience was in an uproar as the horse took off at full speed, this time not stopping until the jester was back through the starting gate and out of sight.

The audience cheered and applauded enthusiastically, clearly pleased with the performance. Julia and Antonius clapped along while Eris smirked and gave a half-hearted clap.

"An amazing race! This calls for another cup of wine…." Eris said sarcastically as she motioned for the servant.

* * *

Opilio had decided to attend the games at the behest of one of his more prominent clients in the city. It was a polite invitation to be at a place where business would not be the primary concern, but a place to socialize and, Opilio hoped, meet new clients. He brought along Thrax and Soroush, as there would not be much going on in the city outside the hippodrome today anyway. Their seats were right along the wall at the edge of the track, not far from the *Kathisma,* where the Emperor and his guests would watch the races.

Opilio would feign interest in the outcome of the races. But between each contest, he did his best to fraternize amongst the well-to-do in attendance. Thrax was more interested in the races than in socializing. Soroush was rather indifferent. His mind was elsewhere. He exhaled deeply and surveyed the amphitheater, looking around tier by tier. His eyes came to a rest up and behind him, on the detailed adornments of the Emperor's lodge. Over the edge of the half-wall enclosing the *Kathisma,* he caught a glimpse of a beautiful woman with golden blonde hair, laughing, drinking, and chatting with someone near her.

His attention was brought back toward the arena as the charioteers began lining up at the starting gate for the next race. A few moments later, the race was underway, and the stadium was again enveloped in a cloud of dust. The crowd roared, Thrax among them. Soroush looked at the giant seated next to him with mild disdain. He could not see the point of these races. To him, they were little else but a distraction. A way to pass the time, even though he did not wish to waste time. But to Thrax, they seemed to be a real delight. Soroush shook his head, resolving to endure the remaining races in silence.

* * *

The sun was nearing the horizon, its reddening hue darkened even more by the dust hanging in the air. The final heat of charioteers was underway, and the crowd was in a frenzy. This final race would break the three-to-three tie between the Blues and Greens. As the chariots rounded the turn into the final lap, the entire Hippodrome was shaking from the thousands in the stands jumping and shouting. A charioteer trailing a green flag and whipping his horses furiously overtook a blue charioteer on the last stretch and won the race to an explosion of cheers from the onlooking citizens.

The races were now complete, and an air of elation hung over the crowd. After the dust settled, seven men carrying ram's horns emerged from the gates and fell into formation. They held their horns in the air and together sounded a mighty blast that heralded the victors. The crowd cheered again as the victors were marched in on foot from the entrance gate. They made their way to the *Spina* and climbed on top, standing shoulder to shoulder.

The patrician Bonus entered the arena carrying seven laurel crowns. He was followed by a page pulling a small cart laden with a wooden chest. The crowd cheered as Bonus presented each winner with a laurel crown. The winners bowed to the stands on each side. Bonus gestured to the page who opened the chest sitting in the cart. From it, the page produced seven large pouches filled with coins, which he passed up to Bonus, who handed the pouches on to the winners. Bonus applauded the winners one last time and then led them out of the arena. Another blast of the ram's horns signaled the official end of the games.

The Greens, known as the people's team, had emerged victorious today, and Antonius could sense a celebratory mood in the Hippodrome. Hopefully, the positivity would remain as the crowds returned to the city.

He turned and spoke to Eris and Julia, "Ladies, it has been a pleasure spending the day with you. However, I must return to my duties. If you need me for anything, please speak to Isaac. He will know where to find me."

Eris laughed. "So formal, Antonius. Are you sure you don't want to stay? What are we supposed to do with ourselves?" Her words were full of wine, so much so that Eris herself laughed at the way they sounded.

Julia graciously interposed. "Please, Antonius, we know you have to go. I will accompany Eris on her way home. Thank you for such a lovely time."

"Yes, yes, yes. A *very* lovely time," Eris added, giggling. Antonius could only smile. Bowing his head slightly, he departed.

Opilio, Thrax, and Soroush stood along with most of the crowd, readying to depart the Hippodrome. As Opilio continued his efforts to mingle, Soroush took another look around the amphitheater, admiring again the Emperor's Lodge and the beautiful woman seated there. She was standing now, with her back turned, next to another woman. She swayed to the side, and a man's face came into view. Soroush froze, incredulous. *Could it be?* he thought to himself.

His hand wandered up to his chest and found the leather cord around his neck. He gripped the jackal's tooth tied to the cord and began rolling it between his fingers as he stared up at the man. *Yes.* This was him—the strong jaw, the dark eyes. Soroush felt his heart begin to beat heavily in his ears, and his hands began to tremble. It took every ounce of his willpower to remain composed.

Of all places, he thought. But why not? The man he sought was a Roman officer, after all. Soroush watched as the man excused himself and walked out of the Emperor's Lodge, leaving the two women behind.

He reached out and tapped Opilio's arm, saying, "I will return to the ship tomorrow."

Opilio looked somewhat confused but said nothing and nodded in agreement before rejoining the conversation he was having with one of the spectators.

Thrax watched as Soroush's gaze returned to the blonde girl in the *Kathisma*. Laughing heartily, he slapped Soroush on the shoulder and said, "Good luck!"

"I will return tomorrow," repeated Soroush, and he set off up the stairs of the amphitheater toward the Emperor's lodge as Thrax made exaggerated kissing noises at his back.

*　*　*

The sun had sunk well below the horizon by the time Antonius was done with his duties at the Hippodrome. He made his way back to his quarters and entered, unsure of what he ought to say to the Persian girl he had left alone inside. He carried fresh fruit, bread, and water with him. Surely she was hungry by now. He removed his breastplate and cape and laid them on his bed. Taking a deep breath, he walked slowly up the stairs in the corner. As he opened the door, he saw his Persian captive sitting on the hard floor, staring at him.

He cleared his throat. "I had hoped to return sooner. Here, eat." He handed her the fruit and gave her the decanter of water he had brought with him. He was not quite sure what he expected her to say, but the girl simply began to eat the foods he brought her, saying nothing. "My name is Antonius."

"Asana," the girl said, not looking up from her meal.

Antonius stepped backwards as if to leave but stopped short. He stood at the entrance to the tower room, shrouded in a heavy silence. Asana took notice and ceased eating, intrigued now by what the pensive Roman might say. And, for the first time, she took notice of how handsome he was. The masculine angles of his tanned face were softened by his short, thick dark hair. His eyes shone with an inner brightness. Their brown opals were streaked with bands of green and gray. His handsomeness was understated, and his face masked a quiet intensity that Asana could sense, pulsing under his stoic expression.

Antonius brought his hand to his neck and stroked the stubble there as he gazed off at nothing in particular.

"When you were in Antioch…" Antonius hesitated. Eventually deciding to continue, he said, "When you were in Antioch, there was a place where they kept the prisoners. A pit."

102

Asana nodded. "Yes, but how…"

"And you would bring food to the prisoners in that pit," he interrupted.

Asana was struck silent. *How could he know that?* she wondered.

"It is true, isn't it?" he asked, looking into her eyes.

"Yes…"

Antonius reached into his tunic and grabbed the thin chain that hung around his neck. Removing the chain, he held it toward her in his outstretched hand, the silver ring hanging from its end, glinting in the dim light of the room. "Then I believe that this belongs to you…"

Asana was astounded. The ring was lost years ago on one of her most dreadful days. Had it really returned to her in the hands of this Roman? She stood and took the ring, studying it intently. The ends of the delicate silver band had been crafted to appear as cypress boughs. These boughs curved to embrace a single stone, a dark jade in the shape of a crescent moon. This was her mother's ring. There could be no doubt now.

Antonius approached her and bent, unclasping the fetter from around her ankle.

Asana was motionless, overwhelmed by the memories the ring evoked. "My *Baba*… father… gave me this ring. He told me that he hired an artisan in India to make it for my mother as a gift. She wore it every day, even on the day she died… the day I was born. When I was old enough, *Baba* told me what had happened to her, and he gave me the ring." Tears ran down her face. She wiped them with her arm and spoke again, this time looking at Antonius. "It was you in Antioch. You were the man at the bottom of that awful pit."

Antonius closed his eyes and bowed his head, answering. "Yes."

"And you lived…."

"Yes, but I now know that I have you to thank for my life. I certainly would have died if not for the nourishment you brought me. Thank you."

In response, Asana only nodded.

"Why?" Antonius asked. The girl's expression became one of confusion, so he added, "Why did you help me? I am the enemy of your people, of your family…."

"The *Ahura Mazda* teaches that we have no enemy except for the one inside of ourselves. I could simply not watch such suffering. *Baba* would try to keep it from me, but at night I could hear the screams and wails echoing through the fortress. It is not right that men should treat one another so cruelly." She looked away, clearly shuddering at the memory of it all.

"But your father… it is his duty to kill Romans. We are at war! You were helping me, a man whose duty it is to kill Persians!"

"So? All of this fighting for years and years. One soldier will not make the difference!"

"I think there are many soldiers who would disagree."

"I am certain. My father, too, would surely disagree. But all of these soldiers who we suppose will make the difference, and yet the war continues. Brothers, husbands, and fathers dying by the hundreds. So, what should I have done? Sent poisoned wine to the bottom of the pit? Rid the world of one more Roman soldier and thus win the war for Persia? I am tired of all the death!"

Antonius was taken aback by the impassioned retort. Hidden deep under his pride and his vengefulness was a part of him that was also tired of the war and the death that it brought. The Empire had been at war for as long as he could remember, and peace seemed like a mirage, always fading away when it was closest. He sighed heavily.

He outstretched his hand, palm up, and said, "Come…."

Asana collected herself and stood, following Antonius out of the tower room and down the few steps into his chamber. They crossed the room, and he opened a door on the far end, revealing a tight stone staircase that spiraled upwards. He ascended and she followed, coming at last to an archway, and from it, a stone balcony spilled out into the night.

There was a breeze, and the cool evening air was a refreshing contrast to the heat earlier that day. The balcony was very high above the ground. It faced north and had an expansive view over the city to the west and east. Nearest to them were the Hippodrome, the *Kathisma,* and the rest of the palace grounds. Beyond that, the city stretched up the hills. Asana beheld the scene reverently. The avenues were lined with apartments and homes and taverns and markets. A vast field of marble, stone, and wood ended at the waters of the Golden Horn to the north and at the massive Theodosian walls to the west. The occasional voices could be heard echoing up toward the balcony, celebrants of the day's festivities still wandering through the streets near the palace.

"It's breathtaking, isn't it?" Antonius asked.

"Truly. Not since I was a girl in Ctesiphon have I seen such a sight."

"I have been living in the palace for more than a year, and I am still awed by this view." Asana watched Antonius as he looked upon the flickering lights of the city. His shoulders relaxed, and a soft smile overtook his lips. He stood peacefully for a while longer before continuing, "When I was a boy in Thessalonica, my father took me on a ship to the markets here in Constantinople...

"The sun was beginning to set when the city came into view. I had always heard about the capital of the Empire, but that was the first time I had seen it with my own eyes. I could not believe that such a magnificent place could exist. The massive walls, the dozens of ships coming and going from the harbors, the marble and brick buildings covering the hills... I remember my father and I standing near the prow of the ship as we approached. He leaned over and spoke into my ear over the noise of the wind, 'My son, there is Byzantium. The new Rome. Constantinople, the Queen of Cities. Nowhere in the world will you find its equal.' Since then, I have been many places... but none have compared."

Asana found herself musing over the deep, calming tone of the Roman's voice. Her eyes were drawn to his lips as he reminisced. But when he turned to look at her, she quickly looked away. "And where is your father now?" she asked.

"He is dead," Antonius said rather abruptly. "He died at the beginning of the war..."

"I see..." Asana replied quietly. Her question had brought a weight into his mind, and his eyes sank toward the floor. She was greatly moved with compassion. Though Antonius maintained a stoic appearance, he could not hide the sincerity of his emotions. Asana could sense he was guarded, lonely. It was as if the man was a deep well from which no one had ever drawn water. She saw in him the same solitary condition she saw in herself, and her empathy began to animate her. Trembling slightly, she took a small step toward Antonius. He turned his eyes to hers, and his confusion gave way to recognition. She quickly took a final step and, closing her eyes, stood tall to reach his lips and kiss them.

For a moment, there was only the feeling of his lips on hers. All the sounds and sights of the city faded into nothing. Even the breeze died off, as though the very air acknowledged the solemnity of their kiss. Asana pulled away and opened her eyes. Antonius was looking back at her. He was taken. The starlight seemed to find a home in the girl's green eyes, and kindled a new brilliance. The two were conscious of the same ineffable feeling that neither had the words to describe. But in their silence, a thousand words were spoken, and in their next kiss, ten thousand more.

Antonius ran his hand down through her hair. Her knees lost their strength as a rush climbed up through her body. His chin was rough with the stubble of his beard, but his lips were deliciously soft. All the pain and anxiety in Asana's heart receded into the background, and for the first time in a long time, she felt calm. Content.

Antonius pulled away, and it felt as though he was waking from a dream. *How did this happen?* He thought to himself. Two days ago, he was diligently performing his duties to the Empire, uninterrupted. Now he felt adrift in uncharted waters. *Is this truly the girl who saved me?* He looked straight up at the stars above, as if the answer might reveal itself in the firmament. But the feeling of her lips kissing his neck pulled him back to Earth.

Their embrace continued, and neither he nor she tired of their introduction. Eventually, he sat down against the stone of the archway, looking at the sky over the city. She sat beside him and put her head on his chest. Soon she fell asleep, lulled by the slow rhythm of his breathing.

Chapter VI
The Moonlit Gardens

Asana woke in confusion. Looking around, she saw that she was in the tower room once more. Though to her relief, there were no chains on her ankle. Had it been a dream? Or had he carried her down here as she slept? Collecting herself, Asana stood and made her way to the door. She found it locked and beat her palms on the heavy wooden door in frustration. Too many thoughts, too many emotions washed over her. Overcome, Asana fell to the ground and wept.

It was foolish to think that anything should have changed, she thought amidst her tears. Often the most intense, transformative experiences happen late in the evenings—dreams, epiphanies… kisses… And often, in the light of day, the force of the experience fades. The *realness* of the experience evaporates alongside the morning dew. After another hour, Asana wondered whether she and the Roman had even kissed at all…

*　*　*

Eris couldn't say when she first started thinking this way, and at first, she felt guilt. Francio had been good to her, and it was not right for a woman to go behind her husband's back. *But Francio is seldom home, and I am lonely,* she reasoned with herself. *And besides, he does not treat me the way a beautiful wife should be treated.*

For days, then weeks, then months, this conversation repeated itself in her head. Neither side of this inner struggle had made a convincing enough argument to lead her to a decision. Until one day, she had learned that Francio was in the tavern drinking with the men just before setting out on the most recent campaign. The wives had a way of being each other's ears, and it had gotten back to Eris that her husband was speaking lewdly about her in public.

She remembered the tales that were told of Empress Theodora, wife of Justinian, and her free lifestyle. Surely, if these sudden fancies were fit for an Empress, then they were fit for her as well. From that moment on, when Eris traveled through the city, she would no longer look forward and go about her business. No, now her eyes would be wandering, looking for someone she had never met but was certain was out there.

He would be young and strong and handsome. He would fall instantly in love with her. How could he not?

Francio took her beauty for granted now. So she stood in front of a mirror, lining her blue eyes and reddening her cheeks in a deliberate way. She set her hair up with pins and put on her necklace and anklets. Satisfied with her work, she set out through the wooden door of her home and into the city.

*   *   *

Antonius arrived back at his quarters mid-morning with more food and water for Asana. He unlocked the entrance to the tower room and stepped inside. He was greeted with the same icy stare he had received the first morning she had awakened in this room.

"Good morning…" Antonius said tentatively.

"It most certainly is not," Asana responded curtly.

Antonius sighed. "Because of the lock…"

"Yes. Because of the lock! Everywhere I have gone for years has been behind a lock. Except for last night. But this morning you were gone, and the lock had taken your place!"

"I did not want to leave you, and I did not want to lock the door, but I had to," Antonius explained.

"Do you intend to keep me in here forever?" Asana asked. "I am a prisoner!"

Her exasperation bled through in the tone of her voice. Antonius knew she was right. But what could be done? There was no place he could bring her in the city that wouldn't put them both in danger. And moving anywhere inside the palace was sure to get them noticed unless all the guards abandoned their posts at the same time… *Or if they were ordered to…*

Antonius clasped his hands and spoke energetically, "I know what we can do. One more day is all I ask while I arrange it. I will see you when I return this evening, and we will leave here for a time."

"And go where?" she asked skeptically.

"You will have to see it with your own eyes."

"And do I have a choice? Or will you be locking the door on the way out?"

"I will leave it unlocked, but you must promise me you will not try to leave."

It was Asana's turn to sigh now. She did not have the energy to argue. Besides, she was in a foreign land. She didn't know anything about the city she was in, and she knew no one except her former captors... *and my current captor,* she thought dryly.

She had nowhere to go. "I promise I will stay here."

"I will return this evening. Please eat. Drink."

* * *

Eris stroked her golden hair more than once to ensure she had the full attention of the young man that she had passed by on the way to the forum. She did her best to make sure a conversation was an inevitability, and sure enough, the handsome stranger approached her.

He spoke Greek but with an accent. This was appealing to Eris. It added an exotic element to her fantasy. He was courteous and soft-spoken. His eyes were piercing and enigmatic. His lithe walk and sharp features would look dangerous were it not for his persuasive, disarming smile.

When he approached, he said, "If I may introduce myself, my name is Soroush."

She did her best to be as flirtatious as possible, and to these flirtations, Soroush was quite receptive.

He offered to walk with her, and they spent the morning in the market. He bought pears and figs from one of the vendors, and the two walked down towards the sea. They ate to the sound of the water lapping at the seawalls. He told her of his home in the east. He told her of the many places he had seen and the many adventures he had as a deckhand on the merchant ship. The evocative way that he described his journeys and his thoughts held Eris' full attention. The Pyramids of Egypt, the Lighthouse of Alexandria, and the Parthenon in Athens.

"You are so young, but you have traveled so far!" Eris fawned.

Soroush shrugged innocently. "We are led where we are led." After more lighthearted conversation and laughter, he stood and said, "I have had a lovely time with you, but I must go. I have work I must do at the harbor."

"Oh, that's too bad. It was so nice meeting you," Eris said, her voice dripping with sweetness.

"Would you do me the honor of meeting me again tomorrow?" Soroush inquired, his dark eyes feigning an eager innocence.

"Yes, I would like that very much."

"In the morning, at the same place?" he offered.

Eris nodded. With a kiss on her hand, Soroush left her with a flutter in her heart and a smile on her face.

* * *

Antonius was pacing back and forth on the marble pavement of the *Augustaion* outside the *Chalke* gate. There were a thousand thoughts and a thousand considerations competing with each other for attention in his mind.

He had sent for Isaac, and sometime later, the young soldier presented himself and saluted. "Yes, sir?"

"I would say this new position suits you well, Isaac."

"Thank you, sir," Isaac responded proudly, a new levity filling his posture.

"I have an assignment for you. As you know, the garrison of the city, indeed the whole army, is short of manpower," Antonius began. Isaac nodded. "Our advantage here is that each man is highly trained, ready, and loyal. But readiness is difficult to maintain behind the walls. The luxury, the people, the food, the races... all of these things tend to relax a soldier. And if the soldiers in a garrison relax, the city is in danger."

"I understand, sir."

"So, I would like to have you take detachments of the men on marches and drills through the city starting this evening. Tonight you will march in formation with half of the palace guard to the Theodosian walls. You will ensure that each guard, and eventually all the soldiers in the garrison, are able to man the battlements proficiently. Have them familiarize themselves with all nine gates and the local commanders at each station. Many of the palace guard have probably not been atop the walls in years."

"Yes, sir. And what of the rest of the palace guard?" Isaac asked.

"You will have the remainder posted evenly around the perimeter of the palace, with an extra six men at the Chalke gate," Antonius answered.

"Yes, sir."

"You will report to me in the morning. That will be all."

"Thank you, sir."

* * *

That evening, when Asana heard him approach the tower door, she did not know what to expect. The door swung open, and Antonius appeared with a mischievous grin.

113

She cocked her head to the side in confusion, and he held out his hand, saying, "Come! There won't be much time."

Antonius led her by the hand through the palace at a brisk pace, pausing only to look around each corner before proceeding. Asana was bewildered. She had only seen his quarters and the view over the city. She had no idea what opulence lay just outside Antonius' door. Marble balustrades, gold leaf columns, massive frescoes, intricate mosaics, and grand statuary slipped by without even a moment for Asana to stop and digest what she was seeing.

"Where are we going?" she asked futilely.

"Shhh," was Antonius' abrupt response.

At last, they reached a large stone archway that opened into a vast courtyard. The marbled hallways of the palace continued as marbled pathways outside. Trees and vines and flowering plants of every kind stretched out in all directions, meticulously maintained. High stone walls enclosed the courtyard on all sides. And high above the walls, the full moon cast its silent glow over it all.

Asana was stunned. "What is this place?" she asked, her voice colored with wonder.

"The Gardens of Byzantium," Antonius said. "Constantine the Great designed these gardens during the construction of the palace three hundred years ago."

He pointed to the right, and Asana's eyes followed. There, on a large stone pedestal, was a marble statue of the great emperor himself, clad in his imperial regalia. The visage of Constantine gazed solemnly down on those entering the garden, hand outstretched, gesturing for them to continue on.

Asana stared at the statue for some time until she felt Antonius take her hand once more. He smiled at her, and they began walking slowly down the garden path. The way was lined with yellow hellebore and purple larkspur, irises of many colors, and crocuses that had not yet bloomed. The air was

114

thickly perfumed by these flowers, and Asana breathed deeply. She felt as though she had stepped into a myth. A sanctuary.

The path continued on toward the center of the courtyard, where there was a circular grove of olive trees.

"The Emperor's own," Antonius explained. "Up the other path are pomegranates, apricots, plums…all kinds of fruit…"

As her eyes were tracing the gnarls in the olive branches, Asana heard the quiet sound of running water. They walked around the olive grove, and she saw that there was a small stream winding its way through the courtyard.

"Amazing…" Asana said reverently, gesturing toward the stream. They approached a stone footbridge that crossed over the water. "I have never seen anything like this."

Pausing halfway across, Asana leaned over the stone rail of the bridge and looked down. The moonlight rippled on the water as it meandered over the rocks of the stream bed. The effect was hypnotic.

"This stream is fed from the aqueducts and cisterns to the west and is used for everything in the palace: water for the soldiers, the horses, and of course, the gardens."

They walked along the path, which now lay between the high wall of the courtyard and the winding course of the stream. Asana stopped as they approached a large mosaic on the wall.

Thousands of small tiles of many colors and materials swirled together to show a mother holding an infant child, a halo around each of their heads. Though made of simple tiles, the expressions on their faces were deeply radiant. The image alone was powerful enough, but when Asana noticed the bed of Persian lilies growing at the foot of the mosaic, tears welled in her eyes. *Of all the flowers,* she thought, wiping her tears away and sniffling.

Antonius' brow furrowed in concern. "What is your trouble?"

"I…" Asana hesitated and exhaled deeply, trying to restrain the quaver in her voice. "It is just… just very touching…"

"Hm," Antonius replied, looking down at the ground. He knew there was something she did not want to tell, did not want to be asked. So they stood beside each other in silence. She with her arms across her chest and him with his hands clasped behind his back. A soft breeze picked up and made its way through the leaves of all the plants in the gardens, carrying with it the scent of citrus and jasmine. Like an invisible hand, it ushered the two onward. They turned and continued slowly alongside the stream. The water's quiet rustle and the whispering wind were the only conversation.

Eventually, they reached the far wall of the courtyard. Here, the stream came to a head. Water poured from a long, narrow opening midway up the wall, falling upon stacked stones. The water flowed off the stones in all directions and tumbled noisily into a pond below. The pond itself was lined with rock, surrounded on all sides by flowers and vines. Antonius stepped forward and knelt, gathering water into his palms and splashing his face.

Asana watched from a few steps away as he rubbed water onto his arms and onto the back of his neck. In a flash, she was struck by a memory from years ago—a dream she had of a man… A man at a lush oasis, kneeling beside the water. A man whose face she was not able to see… She felt foolish when she thought about dreaming of the future. But the image of this Roman at the water's edge… *she had seen this before.*

Her thoughts were interrupted by the realization that he was looking at her. "Are you feeling alright?" Antonius asked.

Asana cleared her throat and said, "Yes." She thought for a moment and then added, "I should like to clean my clothes."

Antonius was confused at first, but realizing it had probably been some time since she had clean clothes, he said, "Oh...of course." Antonius was again confused as she remained motionless, staring at him with her eyebrow raised. "Oh, yes. I will... I will wait there," he said sheepishly, motioning toward a tree a dozen steps away.

Making his way to the tree, he leaned his back against it. He heard the splashing of the water in the pond behind him as he looked up at the glowing moon filtering through the branches.

His mind was adrift, thinking again of how he had arrived at this time and place, musing about what the future might hold. The weary soldier thought of the war, the Emperor, the empire, and the duties he had for the next day. He thought of Isaac, and Eris, and Julia, and Francio, and Urbicus, and of the Persian girl who had come into his life by such a strange twist of fate. A girl he had snuck into the Emperor's own garden. He smiled and shook his head at the absurdity of it all. *Asana...* he said to himself.

"Antonius..."

Her voice startled him. He came out from behind the tree and took one step before stopping. He saw the clothes that were draped neatly over the rocks at the water's edge. And then he saw Asana, standing in the center of the pond, wearing nothing but her copper bangle and armlet. Her long, dark hair was soaked, the water running down her shoulders onto her breasts. Her skin glistened in the moonlight.

Asana waited breathlessly to see what Antonius would do next. He walked slowly toward her, as if giving himself time to reconsider. At the edge of the pond, he removed his shirt and stepped in. She looked upon the muscles and scars of his arms and chest in silence. They told the story of a life defined by war. He took one last step toward her through the water. Asana nearly stumbled backward at the approach of this man, who suddenly seemed so imposing… so *real*. She collected herself and looked up, only to find his eyes staring into hers.

A very curious, unspoken thought passed between them. It felt as though all of their past decisions were not their own but rather the insistent hand of fate pulling them toward this place and this time. Their lives seemed like nothing more than a prolonged anticipation of this very moment, and the anticipation was becoming unbearable. And when she could not bear to resist any longer, Asana surrendered to the will of the moment and kissed him passionately, unreservedly. With one hand on her cheek and the other running through her hair, Antonius kissed her with equal abandon. Their embrace was magnetic.

Asana could feel her heart race and sense its beat even in her toes. Her knees began to quiver, and she wrapped her arms around Antonius' neck to hold herself fast. Her weight moved him not at all. It seemed to her as if he were one of the marble statues in the garden. His hand found the small of her back and urged her closer. Antonius felt his blood rush. He moved his hands across her breasts, and she exhaled deeply. She reached for one of his wrists and guided his hand down to her thighs. And when his finger traced her folds, she shuddered. Asana moved her feet apart to give him room to continue his explorations.

With her hand, she grasped Antonius, feeling him thicken as she squeezed and pulled. His breath quickened, and when he could wait no longer, he lifted Asana, one firm hand under each side of her behind. She wrapped her legs around his back and cradled his head against her breasts. Carrying her, he

118

stepped through the water and over the edge of the pond, kissing her on the way. He bent and laid her on the ground. Leaving her legs locked behind him, Asana reached her hand between their bodies. She grasped him again, finding him firm and unyielding. She traced herself with him for a moment before finally pulling him in.

Antonius was overtaken by a wave of pleasure, her wetness embracing him tightly. Asana inhaled sharply and tensed as her body adjusted to his presence. He slowed his movements until he felt her muscles relax and began moving rhythmically, in time with her. He lowered his head and began climbing her shoulder and neck with his lips. Small blossoms of warmth electrified her skin with each kiss he planted, like flowers unfolding on the vine. Asana savored each one rapturously.

Soon, the first beads of sweat appeared on Antonius' brow from his efforts. His breathing was heavier now, and her moans had taken on a luscious quality that only intensified his want. Asana was possessed by the moment, her pleasure having a force and completeness she had never known before. Her lips found the muscle of his shoulder, and she bit down. The bite caused Antonius to quicken. The tangible euphoria enveloped her and alighted on each nerve, every inch of skin. Before she knew what was becoming of herself, her thoughts were shattered by bright, pulsing cascades of bliss.

For what seemed like ages, the sensation drowned out all else. Until finally, she could hear the beating of her own heart in her ears and then Antonius' heavy breathing and animalistic groan as he was overtaken by pleasure. Exhausted, he collapsed on top of her. Asana relished his closeness, his weight, his warmth. Fully content, she closed her eyes and let herself drift…

* * *

As Asana lay on her back, staring up at the sky, she was ebullient. The emotion came not only from the positive feelings of the moment but also from how much that positivity stood in contrast to the torments of the days and weeks and months that preceded. She could not remember the last time she had felt happiness.

This place, these gardens, gave Asana a sense of familiarity. She knew she had never been here before, but even still, the sensation remained—a warmth in the back of her mind. And while she lay there, her mind returned to the dream she had on that riverbank years ago while fleeing Antioch. The dream of an oasis and a man. A man whose face she did not see, a man she didn't know. Suddenly, her blissful mood began to drain into a cold valley that was unfolding inside her.

Her unease doubled as clouds started to cover the face of the moon, sailing in on a chilled and strengthening breeze. She closed her eyes, but the face of Maren, the old woman, and her fire in Berytus trespassed into her thoughts. Asana felt dread. Dread that climbed up her spine until she could hear the old woman's words again, the words that Asana herself had compelled her to say, *"You have looked upon your true love and not known him once. So you shall do so a second time, still not knowing. And fate is cruel; for when you finally see, it will be through bittersweet eyes for the end will not be far off!"*

She gasped and opened her eyes, her heart now racing.

"What happened?" Antonius asked.

Asana remained silent for a moment, catching her breath before saying, "I was just drifting."

Antonius, seeing the clouds and sensing the tidings of rain, said, "Come, let's return to the palace. The rain is coming, and the guards will be returning soon."

The following Sunday, Isaac was standing in the forecourt of the *Hagia Sophia*, looking out onto the *Augustaion*. The morning's mass had just finished, and the people of the city were filing out of the grand church and milling about the square. They talked quietly and took their time as they made their way up the cobbled avenues and back to their homes.

Isaac was always impressed by this weekly occurrence. A crowd of this size in this city would almost always be loud and boisterous, sometimes even violent. But from the hours-long ceremony and camaraderie of the church service emerged a peaceful throng of citizens, most smiling and all completely devoid of malice. He was pleased. Proud, even. Nowhere in the barbarian lands outside the civilized bounds of the Empire could such a scene be witnessed.

"You are Isaac, yes? We met during the races."

Isaac turned and saw the smiling face who had addressed him by name, though he could not remember hers. "Yes, although I am sorry to say I do not recall your name."

"Julia."

"Yes, of course. What can I do for you, Julia?"

"Well, I was hoping you might know where I could find Antonius," she said, sounding coy.

"On Sundays during the services, he oversees the watchmen in the towers," Isaac replied.

"I see…"

Isaac could sense disappointment in her tone. He asked, "Is there a message you would like me to deliver to him?"

She thought for a moment. "It is perhaps a message I would like to share with him personally."

"Then I shall tell the *tourmarch* that Julia wishes to speak with him," Isaac assured her.

"Thank you, Isaac," Julia said sincerely. But she made no motion to depart, instead lingering in front of the young officer. "Can you tell me, Isaac, why is it that Antonius has not taken a wife? Is it true that he is so dedicated to his work that he has no need of companionship?" Julia could see that her question gave Isaac pause, so she quickly added, "Forgive me. I should not ask you to speak about your commanding officer. I do not wish to cause you any trouble. It is just that my late husband respected Antonius greatly, and I often find myself worrying about him."

Isaac breathed in and exhaled deeply. He brought his hand to his cheek and scratched the small patch of stubble there. "Well… I suspect that he is not in need of companionship."

Julia was paying even closer attention now. "Oh? And why do you think so?"

Isaac was hesitant to say more, but Julia radiated a sincerity that persuaded him to continue. "I have seen the *tourmarch* return to the palace late in the evenings, dressed in civilian clothes. Recently, I have been drilling and marching the men around the walls of the city. I have also occasionally walked the walls of the palace. And from atop the palace walls, I have seen him returning from the gardens with a young woman."

"I see," Julia said faintly. "Well, it is good that he is not alone. Thank you, Isaac. I am sure you have much more important things to do than chattering on with me."

She departed rather abruptly and went on her way. Isaac was left somewhat puzzled. But he was not particularly concerned by her reaction, and his thoughts quickly returned to the masses in the *Augustaion* and to his duties for the day.

*   *   *

Julia sat across from Eris in the courtyard of one of the many wine taverns near the Neorion Harbor. She looked past the other tables and the stone half-wall out onto the avenue that led down to the waters of the Golden Horn. There were many people milling about, though. Being Sunday, the crowds were smaller. Men and their wives and children coming from the ferries... old couples going for long walks near the water... a sailor bidding farewell to his love before heading down to the harbor for the next voyage...They all seemed so content.

In her bronze cup was a sweet white wine. The owner of this particular tavern had family in Bithynia and was always able to acquire excellent wine from the region, even as all the other taverns had resorted to cheaper wines from Attica and Thrace. Or so Eris had explained.

While one of Julia's hands held her cup, the other ran idly through her black hair as she stared off into the distance. Eris was watching her with a smirk, and Julia laughed when she realized she was being observed. "Julia, I have known you for some time, and I must say you seem quite far away today."

"Yes, I suppose I am," Julia replied.

Eris sipped her wine then asked innocently, "Well? Are you going to tell me where you have wandered off to?"

Julia smiled halfheartedly. "Everywhere I look, families are happy together, and I have nothing. Every day, I think about what life would have been like if Urbicus had lived. I think about what our children would have been like. But he has gone from me. Forever. I am alone, and nothing will bring him back. I think to myself, perhaps it is time for me to join the monastery."

Eris listened sympathetically to her friend. She put her hand across Julia's knee and said, "I know Urbicus was a

123

strong and honorable man, and doubtless your children would have been strong and honorable too. But I also know that Urbicus would not want you to spend all your remaining days in mourning for him. He would want you to be happy. You are too young to be locking yourself away."

Julia shook her head. "Even if I were to start over, all of the men of the city are gone. Off fighting or already married! I try to see that in my future, but it does not seem possible."

Eris said consolingly, "Now, now. The largest city in the world, even during a war, is certain to have a man for you. You are gorgeous and intelligent. Every bachelor would be pleased just to have you speak with them."

"You are too kind, Eris."

"It is true. I can tell. All the soldiers at the races were practically falling over themselves looking at you. There must have been doz—wait! I cannot believe I did not think of this before!"

"What is it?"

"Antonius!"

"Antonius?"

"Yes! He has no wife. He is very handsome," Eris said alluringly. "He is an officer, very brave, and well respected," she added for good measure.

Julia sighed. "Well..."

Eris leaned forward excitedly. "Yes?"

"Perhaps I shouldn't be saying so, but I believe Antonius may be involved with someone..."

Eris inhaled sharply, leaning back and putting her hand to her chest, mouth agape. After a moment, her open mouth transformed into a half-devious smile, and she quietly commanded, "Tell me..." She picked up her cup and brought it to her lips, her stare not leaving Julia for an instant.

Julia laughed and then whispered across the table, "I have heard that Antonius has been going for long walks in the

124

palace gardens with a girl while the soldiers are out doing drills."

"Ha! I do not believe it! How did you find out?" Eris asked.

"Oh, I do not want to bring trouble to anyone. But I believed him."

Eris pointed at Julia. "So it was a *he* who told you!"

"Eris, stop it!" Julia laughed, taking another sip from her cup. The laughter was coming easier now, and the warmth of the wine in her belly was bubbling into a pleasant lightheadedness.

"Oh, come on! I never thought Antonius did anything but work. I have to know!" she implored.

"It does not matter who told me. The point is that Antonius, like all the other good men, is taken!" Julia said matter-of-factly.

"Hmph!" Eris said, feigning annoyance.

"You are so lucky, Eris, to have found a husband like Francio," Julia said, changing the subject.

"Yes," Eris agreed, a slight pang of guilt creeping up her throat. She took another drink of wine to wash it away and cast her eyes down at her hands. "Well, the sun is setting. Maybe we should start making our way back."

"Yes, that is a good idea," Julia agreed.

* * *

Eris lay nude on her bed, catching her breath. She was sprawled beside her naked, tanned paramour. The exhilaration was still tangible, her body still trembling. The intensity had caught her off guard. She wondered why the encounter was so exciting to her. Was it because this was forbidden? Or was it simply because this was new? Maybe it was just the strength and vigor of Soroush himself in the throes of passion. Eris concluded that no matter the cause, she wanted the affair to continue. How would it be next time? Was it possible that next time would be even better?

Soroush sat up on the side of the bed, small beads of sweat shining between his shoulder blades. He became conscious of Eris' stare, so he turned to her and kissed her again. He looked into her eyes and felt a sort of cruel satisfaction at how easy it was to ensnare this Roman woman. There was only one reason he was spending any time with the woman at all, and that was to find the Roman officer he had seen Eris with at the races. For Soroush, the momentary carnal pleasures that crossed his path on the way to his objective were simply a nice bonus. And for Soroush, the sincere emotion felt by this woman was irrelevant.

Reminded of his own goal, he suggested as innocently as he could manage, "You know, most of my time in this place has been spent in the harbors. Perhaps we could go for a walk, and you can show me what else can be seen in the city?"

"Of course, darling," Eris said with her sing-song voice. "We can go anywhere you want."

The two took their time getting ready, but by mid-morning, they had left the cool interior of Eris' apartment and gone out into the heat of the day. As they walked down the dusty avenue, Eris did her best to point out everything that might be of interest. She explained that the carved figure at the top of the massive column in the forum was the city's founder, Emperor Constantine. She named the various minor churches and palaces that seemed to reside on every road. She showed him the aqueduct of Valens and the massive cisterns that it fed. "This aqueduct begins many miles away in Thrace and ends in the gardens of the palace," Eris said.

But it was not until they reached the massive splendor of the *Hagia Sophia* that Eris sensed any reaction at all from

Soroush. "I have seen this building before when I was on my way to the races. It is perhaps the most magnificent I have seen in all the world." They gazed upon the dome of the great edifice for some time before Soroush turned to survey the other buildings around the *Augustaion*. The columns and arches of the baths of Zeuxippos at the opposite end of the square would have been awe-inspiring in their own right were they not overshadowed by the great church.

Their attention was drawn to the palace at their left as the clattering of the bronze gate broke the relative quiet. Two columns of soldiers marched through the gate and arrayed themselves in formation. A few moments later, another young soldier made his way out and stood in front of the ranks. What came next curled the corners of Soroush's mouth into a fiendish grin.

Emerging from the opened maw of the palace was the Roman, fully dressed in his officer's uniform. Soroush was transfixed, watching intently as the Roman spoke first to his young deputy and then to the assembled troops.

His focus was only broken when Eris jabbed her elbow into his rib, saying, "Is something wrong?"

"No, I uh… I am just fascinated by the soldiers. These are the palace guards, yes?"

"Yes. As a matter of fact, the man giving the orders is the *tourmarch* of the entire city. Antonius."

Antonius… Soroush weighed and repeated the name in his head as he watched the *tourmarch* drill his troops. For so many years, this Roman had been nothing but a haunting memory, a nameless villain sitting comfortably in the back of Soroush's mind, out of reach. But now this villain had a name. And now this villain was almost within his grasp. "You know this man?"

Eris nodded, saying, "Yes, he served alongside my hus… uh… my cousin. He was kind enough to seat my friend and me with him in the *Kathisma* during the races."

"That is quite the honor! Perhaps this officer intends to become close with you…."

Eris looked at Soroush, surprised. "Oh, no, no. He is nothing more than my friend." There was a moment of silence before Eris continued. "Besides, I've heard that he has a girl who he has been taking for walks in the palace gardens."

"I see," Soroush said quietly. "The Roman soldiers may bring whomever they wish into the palace?"

"Well, the officers who live in the palace may," Eris explained.

Soroush wore a look of incredulity. "Lives in the palace? The Romans are so rich. I should have known that even the officers of their army live in the palaces!"

"Ha! Maybe true, but Antonius lives modestly, even in the palace. Still very much a soldier, from what I see."

"Hm…"

Soroush, for the first time, felt a sense of respect for his adversary. He was somewhat surprised at the realization but reasoned that there is no glory in hunting rabbits. No, it was much better, much more glorious, to hunt a lion. Besides, no amount of respect was going to make him think twice about killing the Roman. Soroush felt Eris' hand on his back.

She had a concerned, inquiring look on her face, so he faked an exhausted smile. "I am sorry, darling. I guess I am more tired than I realized. I should rest. I have much to do at the harbor tomorrow."

* * *

Later in the afternoon, Soroush made his way back toward the harbor of Theodosius, where the ship was docked.

He decided to stop at an inn to have a drink while he thought things through. He swirled the crimson liquid in his cup idly and stared at the knots in the wooden table while his mind worked. After the day's walk, any remaining doubts in his mind were erased. He was certain. He would not ever forget the Roman's face, even if he wanted to. And how fortunate that the lovely Eris was so familiar with the man. Now, at least, he knew he was in the right place.

But how does one kill a Roman garrison commander in the middle of the Great Palace and escape with one's life? Byzantium was the center of Roman power, and the city was swarming with Roman soldiers. The citizens of the city were skeptical of all Persians, a natural result of centuries of warfare. The palace itself was a nearly impenetrable fortress. To complicate matters further, the Great Palace was in a city that was surrounded by the Theodosian walls, which had never been breached. In addition to the massive land walls, the remaining three sides of the city were surrounded by seawalls and defended by the world's most powerful navy.

No, it would be impossible to kill the Roman commander without being seen or captured. Soroush sat and thought, staring into his wine. He had been waiting for the opportunity to drive his blade through the heart of this Roman for many years. He had imagined his revenge down to the smallest detail. He would introduce himself right before the killing so that the Roman would know exactly who ended his life. He would watch as the life drained from his eyes and then spit on his lifeless body, just as the Roman had done to his father. Unfortunately, it looked like killing this Roman directly would be out of the question. But how then could it be done?

Soroush looked out into the forum of Arcadius. The stone plaza was bustling with activity, with citizens passing by and merchants selling their wares. There were grain merchants, men selling fruits, wines, and cloths, while others sold livestock. There were even entertainers performing for the crowds of passers-by. One man sat on a blanket and played a small pipe to a snake that weaved left and right to the melody. An asp. *That would work,* Soroush thought to himself.

But there was still the problem of ensuring the Roman crossed paths with the snake. After many fantastic and impractical musings, he was nearly resigned to giving up on the idea. But Eris' sweet voice emerged from his memory, *"This aqueduct... ends in the gardens of the palace...."*

Of course! he thought triumphantly. A malevolent grin cracked across Soroush's face. He laughed quietly to himself, feeling uplifted as he finished off his wine.

Chapter VII
Distant Thunder
(June of 626 A.D.)

It was early summer when the rumors began. At first, the conflicting reports from the sailors and travelers spoke of Persian forces somewhere in the east. This provoked no reaction at all from the citizens of the capital, as there had been Persian armies wandering the East for decades now. Surely, wherever they were, Emperor Heraclius was certainly not far behind, ready to give battle.

But the next week, the shapeless rumors began to take a more focused form. A Persian army of tens of thousands of men was marching west toward the imperial capital, and Emperor Heraclius was nowhere near. More rumors surfaced, this time of an even larger army: a barbarian horde of Avars and Slavs approaching from the west, preparing for a coordinated assault with their Persian allies.

When these reports first reached Antonius, he dismissed them. "Impossible," he had told Isaac. "Not since Atilla have the barbarians assembled such a force."

"Yes, sir, but this is what we hear, often now, from the riders approaching the walls," Isaac explained.

Antonius rubbed his chin and considered the information at hand. "And when was the last report we had from the field?"

"It has been weeks, sir."

Antonius nodded. "Bring twelve riders to the harbor and send them across the Bosphorus to Chalcedon. There, they are to split into six pairs and ride east by six different routes until they can see the Persian army with their own eyes. Send them immediately."

"Yes, sir."

"And make sure that all the men know every inch of the walls!"

"Yes, sir."

*　*　*

Asana could sense Antonius' frustration when he returned in the evening. His brow was furrowed, and he was rubbing the back of his neck with his hand. She watched as he paced back and forth for a time before she intervened.

"Antonius..." His pacing continued unabated. "Antonius," she said louder. "What is the matter?"

He stopped, looked up at the ceiling, and inhaled deeply. "There are rumors of armies marching on Constantinople."

"Are they true?" she asked.

"I intend to find out."

"So, what will you do now?"

"That is what I am trying to decide," he said curtly.

He resumed pacing, his shoulders weighed down by the burdens in his mind.

To this, Asana could not think of anything to say. His agitation was not going to be reasoned away with words.

So instead, she stood and took hold of Antonius' hand and said, "Take me in the garden."

Her assertiveness caught him off-guard, interrupting his racing thoughts. He saw an eagerness in her eyes that was new and deliciously seductive. He could not resist.

They hurried through the halls of the palace and back to the gardens, where he soon found that her assertiveness was not limited to words. When they arrived at the fountain, she pulled at his clothes, urging him to undress. Her one hand grabbed hold of his belt, pulling it away from his abdomen, and her other hand reached inside with no fanfare or hesitation. She found him full and becoming fuller. With him in her grasp, she led Antonius forward a few steps toward the edge of the fountain pool. She bent at the waist and placed her hands on the pond's edge to support herself.

Antonius wasted no time and was quickly inside her. Asana bit down on her lip, savoring the delicious intensity of his entrance. At first, she moved with him to slow the force of his aggressive thrusts. Then, as she caught up to his pace and relaxed, she moved against him, urging him with her body to become more aggressive still.

His hands strengthened their grip on her hips, and she arched her back. The warmth of his breath on her shoulder gave way to the pleasurable sting of his teeth sinking into her skin. Asana inhaled sharply as he bit her again, further up her shoulder. *I brought this out of him,* she thought with satisfaction. That this man, who seemed always poised and professional, had been overtaken by his inner animal was exciting to Asana. Many may have seen this animal on the battlefield, but few, she imagined, had seen him like *this.*

She had no time to dwell on the thought. His next motion sent intoxicating chills through her body, trapping her in the moment. She felt his rhythm building toward the inevitable. Closing her eyes, Asana let herself be overcome. Waves of warmth were growing and intensifying. Her legs began to shake in anticipation. He was unrelenting, and she found herself helpless to delay. A quiet, primal moan beyond her control came from within. A burst of light filled her mind's eye, and the sounds of the surrounding garden were drowned out as she enjoyed the waves rushing through her. Her body tensed and relaxed over and over, her heartbeat heavy in her ears now, her breathing rapid and shallow.

Antonius followed a few moments later, uttering animalistic groans interspersed with satisfied, exhausted laughs. He tried to step away but found his legs weak. He staggered off to the side, catching his weight on the stones around the pond. As he was doubled over regaining his breath, he looked at Asana, who was looking right back at him, smiling mischievously.

"Again?" she asked.

"Ha!" he exclaimed between ragged breaths. "Of course… in a …. moment… or two…"

* * *

134

As they lay recovering from their exertions, they heard a subtle sound. At first, it seemed like the wind was whispering through the leaves. Yet Antonius and Asana looked at each other questioningly, as if to ask the other whether the sound was imagined. As they wondered, the sound came again, this time more clearly. No, not the wind. Not the wind at all... It was a hiss.

It was the ancient, paralyzing hiss that every man, woman, and child instinctively feared. It was the hissing of a serpent. The two sat up slowly and saw a black and green asp coiled not far from their feet. The snake's callous, predatory eyes were trained directly on them. Its shimmering neck swayed slowly and hypnotically from side to side. Asana shuddered, exhaling in near panic.

"Move back..." Antonius whispered.

But she was too petrified to move. He put his hand on the small of her back, and only then did she slowly draw her legs toward her, though she was shaking visibly.

Antonius reached behind him with his other hand, searching for anything that would be to his advantage against this inhuman foe. He slowly drew his legs in, but the asp struck. A lightning flash of its ivory fangs and pale pink maw was accompanied by a sharp, loud hiss. The fiendish creature fell just short, its jaws closing on nothing. Antonius had his legs under him now and was on one knee. Asana had scurried backward until her back stopped against the stones around the pond's edge. Antonius inched backwards, still searching with his hands, his eyes locked on the snake. The snake unwound from its coil, slowly this time, as it began to close the gap between itself and the hapless pair before it.

Antonius' left hand found his tunic lying on the ground where Asana had discarded it. His right hand found a stone the size of his fist. He was inching his hands forward when the serpent struck again. Instead of finding flesh, the coiled asp had pierced the cloth of the tunic that Antonius managed to bring forward in time. Entangled and trapped by its own fangs, the asp writhed madly in its efforts to free itself. Antonius quickly brought the tunic to the ground. Pinning the snake with his left hand, he brought the rock in his right hand down on its ensnared head, causing an initial brutal *crack* followed by repeated thuds until there was no life remaining.

Antonius exhaled a sigh of relief and looked at Asana, who was still trembling wildly. "We are alright." He tried to assure her. She said nothing. Taking her face in his hands, he looked at her eyes, but she stared, unblinking, off into the distance. "Asana…"

"Are there… many snakes here?" She sounded almost childlike in her fear.

"No. This is the only one I have seen. Come. Let's go back."

* * *

Antonius paced the *Augustaion,* reliving the encounter with the serpent over and over. Never before had he seen a snake in the palace gardens. But then again, never before had he spent so much time there… *No. It is impossible…*

Isaac ran at full speed toward Antonius. He came to a stop and bent, breathing heavily.

"Collect yourself," Antonius instructed while preparing for whatever bad news Isaac might deliver.

"Two-thousand men…. Two-thousand men from the Emperor's army… approach from the east, sir."

"What? Are you sure?" Antonius asked, dumbfounded.

"Yes, sir… A vanguard from the detachment arrived in Chalcedon late in the night… They are ferrying across the river now."

"To the Harbor of Julian?"

"Yes, sir."

"I shall meet them there." Antonius decided. "Send word to Bonus and Sergius that our Emperor has provided reinforcements."

"Yes, sir." Isaac pivoted on his heel to carry out the order.

Antonius made his way down to the harbor, flanked by two of the palace guards. The heat of the late morning sun dissipated in the breeze as they neared the water. He arrived at the harbor as the men stationed at the docks were mooring a small ferry and assisting the others in stepping off the humble vessel. The soldiers were greeting each other warmly, clasping forearms in the common and ancient manner of Roman legionnaires.

He was pleased to see the positive effect the new arrivals were already having on morale. A glimpse of one of the faces stepping out of the boat triggered a sense of familiarity in Antonius. He stepped forward to get a better look, and in a flash, he recognized the face of his old friend.

"Francio!" Antonius barked.

Francio looked up, startled. "Antonius?" The two embraced, smiling widely. "I didn't think the *tourmarch* left the palace anymore!" Francio joked.

"Only to clean up the riffraff that washes up in my harbors. The way you look, you'll kill more Persians with your stench than your sword!"

Francio laughed at this. "You might be right, Antonius, it was a long ride, and we men don't get to relax in the baths all day!"

Antonius studied Francio's face. The lines were a little deeper, and the skin was a little rougher. A scar now marked his jaw, and the hair on his head showed hints of gray. *Even after campaigning for years out in the desert, he looks better than he did back in Antioch*, Antonius thought.

"I am glad to see you in command here." The warmth of Francio's greeting was soon replaced by a much more somber tone. "Antonius... Emperor Heraclius has been maneuvering around three different Persian armies in Syria, Armenia, and Anatolia. He engages and defeats one army but must retreat to avoid being trapped by the second and third. Now, the Emperor stands at the very frontiers of Persia, threatening Ctesiphon itself! They cannot break his army apart, so they have ordered one of the Persian armies to head toward Constantinople, hoping the Emperor will give chase."

"So, the rumors of an army marching west are true...." Antonius said quietly. Francio nodded. "How many?"

It was Francio's turn to speak quietly, "Many. Maybe thirty thousand."

"May God help the Romans..." Antonius replied wryly. "That's not the worst of it..." he added. "The Persians have sent emissaries to the *Khagan* of the Avars, inviting them to join the assault on the city."

"We have heard that rumor as well."

"Rumor or not, the *Khagan* hardly needs an invitation," Antonius continued. "The Avars will jump at any chance to sack and plunder this city. The riches of Constantinople are what every brigand and barbarian dreams of when they are sleeping in their cold, bare huts."

"Mm," Francio concurred, nodding.

"Does the Emperor intend to send more men?" Antonius asked.

"As it stands, the Emperor's army is already outnumbered in the field. The two thousand arriving in Chalcedon were as many as could be spared."

"So, three Persian soldiers plus some barbarians for each Roman on the walls. Not the most favorable odds...." Antonius mused.

"Well, I am sure the *tourmarch* of our glorious capital has been busy preparing the defenses. Between baths, of course...."

Francio laughed at his own wittiness, but Antonius could only manage a smile. He motioned for the five men of the vanguard to follow him, saying in a loud voice, "Come. We have much to do." Antonius thought for a moment before adding, "And stop by the baths. Clean yourselves up!"

Francio smiled. "Yes, sir!"

* * *

"That many? Hmm..." Opilio tugged slowly and repetitively at the dry tuft of beard at his chin. "If that is true, we are going to have some problems."

He stared over the edge of the ship into the water as if expecting his reflection to offer the solution.

"We will know soon if it is true," Soroush replied, "and with an army that large, they are sure to succeed." Opilio scoffed, and Thrax shook his head dismissively. Soroush cocked his eyebrows and stared at the pair. "What? You think the Persians will be defeated?"

"Listen, boy," Opilio started. "You are young, and you are from the East, so you may not be familiar with the history of this place. Since the Emperor Constantine made Byzantium the capital of the Empire, this city has *never* been conquered. The land walls to the west are the strongest ever constructed by man. So renowned are they that Atilla the Hun himself did not even make the attempt to overcome them. Indeed, it took three massive earthquakes to do the walls any harm at all. So, I would not assume that the Persians will march into the city at their leisure and without difficulty. There will be hunger, there will be pain, and there will be much blood before we will know who will end up sitting on the throne."

Soroush considered these words and scratched at his collar, feeling the leather cord and the jackal's tooth that were bound around his neck. "I can understand why you believe this. But you are old, and you are from the West. The strength of the Romans is not what it was decades ago when you began your business. If it were, there would not *be* any armies marching toward the city! And these Persian armies are vast. I have seen them! They are no tribesmen like Atilla and his Huns. They have taken countless cities, despite their walls, and they will not stop until they take this city too."

Opilio shot a glance at Thrax as they were both digesting this unexpected retort.

"*Hmph...*" Opilio began rubbing his hands anxiously and stared off to the east over the waters of the Propontis at the shore of Anatolia. He envisioned Persian armies crossing the water, sacking the city, and seizing his ship and his fortune along with it. He shook his head vigorously to banish the image of his gold being divided amongst the Persian soldiers. "So, we will not know until it happens!" he blurted.

"But we will help the Romans?" asked Thrax in his lumbering voice.

"Of course not, you oaf!" Opilio screeched. "We will do nothing until the outcome of the battle is no longer in doubt. Then we shall side with the winner. We will avoid the messiness of this war. Leave that to the peasants! All of these blathering fools, Romans and Persians alike, fighting and dying for and against each other. They think nothing of giving up every comfort and bearing burdens across the deserts and mountains for years at a time on endless campaigns... and for what? For such imaginary things as honor and duty... no, it is all tripe! They will throw their lives away, and we will continue on as always. If the Romans and Persians want to kill each other, we will sell them the weapons! If they want to waste their days in drunkenness, we will sell them the wine! And if this city burns to the ground during the fighting, we will cast off and sail for the next port, where there are surely more fools waiting to buy what we sell!"

Thrax fell back into his usual silence, satisfied with this explanation. Soroush, however, felt revolted by Opilio's admission. Though he had never admired Opilio, he had a sense of appreciation and tentative respect for his employer. Now, that respect had disappeared entirely. One could respect their enemies despite different loyalties, but who could respect a man with no loyalties at all? Opilio was reduced to the stature of a worm in Soroush's mind, a worm who feasted on the corpses it helped create. Soroush resolved to bite his tongue for now. The merchant had always been simply a means to an end, and now it would be that much easier to cast the scheming Cappadocian aside when it became necessary.

"Well, I suppose we must remain ready to sail at a moment's notice…." Opilio said, calmer now. "Why don't you two head below deck and secure whatever cargo is loose? I have a feeling that the Persians will be arriving any day."

* * *

From her perch high in the palace, Asana fought with her own anxiety. She paced Antonius' quarters restlessly, periodically gripping and squeezing her fingers in a futile effort to dispel the worry shading her thoughts. Though she had only known him for a short while, she had sensed a seriousness in Antonius the evening before. He had been quiet and detached. It was as though his mind was racing, sifting through an unending stream of thoughts, looking for an answer that might not come. She rubbed his neck and tried to soothe him, but she found that his worry was contagious.

He is the commander of the garrison… if he is worried, then I am right to worry too… She ran through hundreds of possibilities in her mind, but her thoughts and reasoning became circular, and so she paced the room, waiting. Except that waiting was not good enough. So she paced some more. Asana lifted her head, and her eyes came to rest on the small desk and chair in the corner of the room. On the wooden desk were a small pile of papers, a jar of ink, and a stylus. She recalled seeing Antonius sit and write for brief moments, though she never questioned him as to what he wrote.

Perhaps the source of his worry was in his writing? Did he write notes to himself? Letters containing orders for subordinate officers to carry out? *Maybe it is simply supply lists…* She recalled that the paper in Antioch was used to keep track of food, weapons, and horses. She shuddered as the very thought of Antioch conjured up images that invaded her mind—flames, fighting, and screams. She tried to cast off the memory of that horrible night as soon as it arose, because with it came thoughts of Bahram… and her beloved *Baba. Baba…*

Asana shook her head vigorously, expelling the past from her thoughts, and returned to considering the question at hand. *I cannot bring myself to look at his papers. It would be a betrayal. I will simply ask Antonius to tell me when he returns.* She was content with this resolution for a few seconds. She stopped pacing for a moment and chewed the end of her fingernail. *But if the situation is dire, he would not tell me. He would think he was protecting me.* She began pacing again.

At last, she surrendered. Her curiosity, her anxiety, and her reasoning had aligned themselves and defeated her restraint. She crossed to the desk and gazed down at the ivory parchment. Asana took a moment to admire his handwriting.

142

Black, angular strokes of the stylus crossed the page, evenly spaced and neatly arranged. It seemed that she was pleased by everything about this Roman. There was not a thing about him that she found disagreeable. *But do I admire him because I love him? Or do I love him because I admire him?* Before she considered the answer to her own question, she was startled by her own admission…

I love him…

She shook her head, again expelling a distracting thought as she looked past the handwriting to the words themselves. Asana saw that the writing was neither supply lists nor letters to a subordinate, but rather prose… a poem actually…

Distant Thunders

In the meadows at the forest's edge,
at the rocky damps near restless streams,
Past the pasture's furthest brambled hedge,
in the waxing moments of fearsome dreams,
I, from on the mountain's dusted ledge,
Could see their columns; their helmet's gleams

Warcry greetings, shook tanned canyon walls,
As glinting spearpoints, filed grimly through,
Wardrums beating, in step with greaved foot-falls,
Until night appoints, by its fading hue
The time of meeting, when the owl calls,
Where the priest anoints, burning Syrian Rue,

After solemn silence, as one voice they say
"Onward to the walled jewel of the West,"
Then in a hush, eagerly they pray
The watch is then set, the others; they rest,

And soon upon the breaking of day
Onward they thundered, like waves set to crest

She reflected on the words, rereading them carefully.
He fears the city will fall. He sees it in his dreams... Asana
thought to herself. The realization brought renewed worry. She
looked through the other papers, hoping to find more insight.
She was surprised at how prolifically he wrote.

Many pages were filled entirely with written
quotations:

*Dwell on the beauty of life. Watch the stars, and see
yourself running with them—Marcus Aurelius*

Something about the words resonated within her,
though she couldn't say why. She thought of the seven stars of
the *Parvin* and mused how she indeed watched the stars and
dwelt in their beauty. Soon, Asana was engrossed in the
writings on the desk. Antonius had such depth, but it was depth
that he seldom shared. Her admiration for him grew. She felt
impatience at his absence and yearning for his return.
Quotation after quotation she found amidst the pages:

*But certainly there is nothing better, or more excellent,
or more beautiful than the world – Cicero*

Sometimes, even to live is an act of courage - Seneca

*Accept the things to which fate binds you, and love the
people with whom fate brings you together, but do so with all
your heart - Marcus Aurelius*

She felt her eyes well up, though no tears came. It was
not sadness that moved her, but a sense of contentment. For
years she had fought off embitterment. Despairing at the
misfortunes that befell her and recounting her trials, she had
every reason to despise the world. But she resisted the
temptation, always hoping for better things to come. And now,
reading these words, the world-weary Persian girl felt
ennobled. These voices from the past had reached forward

through time to assure her, to remind her she was right to resist the bitterness, right to embrace life despite its suffering. Exhaling heavily, she placed the papers as she had found them and laid down to rest.

*   *   *

The breathless reports of the imperial horsemen and the merchants still seemed distant in the minds of the people of Constantinople. The war was going well, after all. How could the Persians, after losing so many men to Emperor Heraclius' army, manage to make their way all the way across Anatolia with an army of their own? Were they not almost defeated? Byzantium was the queen of cities, protected by the queen of heaven herself, the Virgin Mary. Unconquered since it was founded by Emperor Constantine, the people of the city had an extra measure of confidence through their faith in God. Surely God would not abandon his people, who were piously seeking deliverance from an army of heathens!

But even the most faithful hearts skipped a beat when the Persian army appeared on the horizon. The fog of rumors dispersed, and the cold reality set in. The Persians encamped at Chalcedon, just across the Bosphorus from Byzantium to the east. When the sun set, the fires of their camps stood out. They were as numerous as the stars in the sky. The flickering glow reached across the river and danced in the wary eyes of the citizens. The people of the city scarcely had time to behold the invading army when the blasts from the ram's horns atop the Theodosian walls to the west were heard. Another army, an army of Avars, was approaching the city, their torches numbering in the tens of thousands.

The soldiers along the walls made ready, but the Avar army did not attack. Instead, they encamped on the plains beyond the walls. The Roman garrison had no rest that evening, and the rising sun illuminated the scale of the danger they faced. Catapults and battering rams, towers, and ladders of every kind were being assembled by the Avars to the west. And to the east, the Persians methodically constructed their ships. Inside the city, every living soul began preparing and praying. Byzantium, the Queen of Cities, was under siege.

Chapter VIII
The Siege
(July of 626 A.D.)

There was already an air of anxiety among the citizens. But the anxiety trebled when word spread that the Avar horde had cut the Aqueduct of Valens and that no more fresh water would be flowing into the city. For as long as they were under siege, the people of Byzantium would have to rely on the water that remained in the massive cisterns and any rain that happened to fall.

Young boys could occasionally be seen climbing the walls to get a look at the barbarians for themselves, only to be shooed away when caught by their mothers or the soldiers. The open-air markets along the avenues of the city were no longer vibrant and festive. Citizens were not buying their food in a leisurely routine manner but were quickly buying what they could, not pausing to haggle or chat. With the city surrounded, the citizens recognized that food would be harder and harder to come by.

The Sunday morning mass at the *Hagia Sophia* was more crowded than usual. The hymns and prayers offered seemed more sincere, more earnest. Many who had not been to mass in years could be seen in the pews, having found a renewed closeness with their creator after witnessing the size of the two armies encircling the city.

In the evenings, the watchfires were now alighted upon the land and seawalls all around the city, and the shouts from atop the walls could be heard constantly. The men hurried back and forth, keeping watch from the battlements, loading stones and arrows up to the parapets. Being outnumbered but not yet under attack drove the men to prepare and strengthen the defenses of the city as much as possible. There was not much time for the soldiers to sleep or eat, but the women, children, and elders of the city dutifully brought food and water to the tireless defenders.

The Patriarch Sergius was seen by all, faithfully walking the entire circumference of the walls enclosing the city, holding aloft an icon of the Virgin Mary, and leading the men in prayer. There was a tremendous sense of unity in the populace. They were all staring down the same impending catastrophe at the hands of heathen barbarians. Old quarrels were forgotten. The food and water were shared freely, and the rich worked alongside the poor. Everyone from all walks of life wanted to contribute to the defense efforts.

Antonius was away by necessity most of the time, directing the defense of the city. When he returned to his chambers late in the evenings, he would rush to embrace Asana. They would kiss passionately and make love in a desperate way each time, as if it would never happen again. They were at the mercy of forces they could not control, and the future was uncertain. The end of everything—the city... the Empire...their very lives... could come at any time. Yet, like a watchfire struggling against a bitter rain, they burned on.

Afterward, they would lay on the floor of his bed chamber where the cool air settled. They would drink wine and feed each other grapes and figs. They lived each moment in an oasis, outside of time and far away from the troubles besieging their minds and the evil besieging the city. Together, legs and arms enrapt, lips and fingers tracing the bounds of the other, they found satisfaction, peace. And though Asana willed the time to halt, it fell ever onwards out of her reach. And each morning, before the sun broke through the windows of the palace, Antonius would don his armor and depart.

* * *

Francio and Isaac stood atop the Theodosian walls, looking out at the vast Avar camp to the west.

"I have never seen an army so large," Francio mused aloud.

Across the rising plain, they could see the barbarians lashing their donkeys to battering rams, mangonels, and catapults. The process took the greater part of the morning, but by midday, the donkeys and their drivers had begun their march down the plain toward the walls with their massive wooden structures in tow. He glanced at Isaac and sensed that, though he was doing his best to conceal it, the young soldier was afraid.

Francio cleared his throat. "Listen. These barbarians are strong. Good fighters. But they will not succeed here."

"How can you be so sure?" Isaac asked.

"Well, they are disorganized. They have not ever attempted a siege before."

"Truly?"

"Yes, it seems that way to me," Francio replied. "As soon as those donkeys reach about midway down the plain, the *Khagan* is going to learn his first lesson about sieges."

"And what lesson is that?"

"Donkeys need armor too."

Isaac smiled as he realized what Francio meant. The archers atop the walls waited until the plodding beasts and the massive wooden siege engines were well within range. An arrow was fired short to trick the Avar drivers into thinking themselves safe outside the range of the defenders on the walls. On they marched, and when enough of the equipment was in range, Francio signaled to the archers to make ready. Soon, with a shout, the order was given, and a hail of arrows rained down upon the poor beasts. Nearly all were killed. There was a panic amongst the drivers who fled back up the plain, leaving everything behind.

Stuck in place with no donkeys to tow them, the siege engines were easy targets. The next volley of arrows was set aflame, their fiery arcs landing on the wooden machines. The barbarian horde encamped on the plain stared helplessly as weeks of effort went up in smoke. The sight of the burning battering rams and catapults elicited cheers and shouts of triumph from the Romans manning the walls. Inside the city, the news spread instantly, and the morale of the citizens greatly improved.

Antonius, too, was pleased with Francio's report of the day's engagement, but his face remained stoic. Antonius knew that the siege was just beginning. There was nothing to celebrate yet. He ordered the men to fully restock the arrows stored in the towers and to ensure that every man had enough water. Francio set off at once to see that this order was carried out. There was no room for error. Every possibility must be prepared for. A single mistake could mean the fall of the entire Empire, and Antonius was not going to allow a mistake.

* * *

Over the next week, a few skirmishes and forays were made by the barbarians at various points along the three-and-a-half miles of wall, but no serious fighting had broken out yet. At the end of the week, the skirmishes ceased. Having learned from his previous error, the *Khagan* of the Avar horde ordered his newly constructed catapults and mangonels to be cautiously positioned outside the range of the Roman archers. Antonius, Francio, and all the men along the walls watched intently as the barbarians loaded the first stone. A solitary, distant shout could be heard. The first catapult was loosed. The massive rock sailed through the air and fell short of the wall, landing with a deep thud. The rock tumbled and skipped forward before splashing into the moat at the base of the outer wall.

The catapult was soon reloaded. The next rock flew higher and, with a tremendous *craaack!* struck the base of the inner wall. Dust and fractured stone shot out in every direction from the wound. Antonius nodded at Francio, who hurried off to oversee the repairs. Mortar and block had been loaded in the towers along the wall in anticipation of these repairs, and all the able-bodied citizens living near the walls had been conscripted to assist in the work. The Patriarch Sergius and the

Patrician Bonus led the citizens, who would also tend to the wounded and ferry water and ammunition when the inevitable assault came.

Now that the barbarians had found their range to the walls, the other catapults and mangonels were loaded. There were nearly a hundred in all. The order went out, and one by one they fired. The loud creak of the wooden catapults and the whip of the mangonels were followed by an eerie silence as the projectiles soared through the air. All up and down the Theodosian walls, the men took cover as the massive stones struck the walls. Jagged, heavy stone shrapnel rained down near the impacts. The Romans hastily began making repairs where the most damage had been done. The walls were well-constructed, and so far, they were holding firm.

Antonius surveyed the accumulating damage and walked to the city side of the walls. Peering down, he was pleased to see the citizens hurrying back and forth, bringing stone, mortar, water, and whatever else was needed to the troops. He was satisfied that he had done everything within his power to defend the city so far, and though the walls were being damaged and a few men were lost, the siege was being dealt with effectively.

He resisted rest and sleep, wanting to keep watch over the walls constantly. No man besides Francio and the Emperor Heraclius himself could have convinced Antonius to retire to his quarters when the enemy was so close. And each evening, Francio persuaded him that the men would suffer if their *tourmarch* was not rested. Antonius would always return with renewed vigor at daybreak to relieve Francio.

* * *

For weeks, Asana noticed a subtle shift in the sounds coming through the window in Antonius' quarters. Though she could not hear the words being spoken, she could hear the tones. Gone was the sound of laughter, the sounds of the shouts of the merchants in the forums. Now, every voice that could be heard spoke in short, abrupt sentences, joyless and direct. Even the birds seemed lacking in their songs.

One evening, Antonius did not return. He had warned her that this was a possibility, as the moon was new and all was dark, so extra care had to be taken to defend against any surprise assaults. Asana fell asleep feeling very much alone. Hours later, she awoke in the pitch darkness to the sounds of men shouting. She could not hear any of the words, but the tone said enough. *Have the walls fallen?* She jumped up and rushed to the spiral staircase, unable to see but navigating by touch. She emerged from the top of the steps onto the stone balcony high above the city. The night air was still hot.

There was a momentary silence. But then, to the east, in the Bosphorus beyond the seawalls, she heard loud crashes and the snapping of heavy timbers. The shouting of men added to the cacophony. Streaks of firelight arced, unmistakable against the abyssal darkness of the water. The flaming streaks seemed to disappear for a moment. But soon, blazing fires blossomed out of the sea. Asana stared in awe. The scene was now illuminated in all its horror for her to behold. Ferries full of Persian soldiers had set out from the opposite shore of the Bosphorus and were attempting to reach the city. Warships flying the *Chi-Ro* flag of the Roman navy were ramming these ferries and setting others alight. Asana could see the silhouettes of unfortunate men who had been caught in the flames leaping into the waters to extinguish themselves.

An hour passed as she stood motionless, watching the conflagration unfold from her vantage point atop the great palace. Thick smoke enveloped the ships, and the blaze reflecting off the surface of the water gave that smoke an ominous glow. It seemed as if hell itself was climbing out of the sea, seeking to swallow the ships and soldiers. The sight alone was horrifying enough. But then the acrid sweetness of burning wood reached her nose. The smell was polluted with the sickly scent of something else...

"Burning flesh..." she whispered to herself.

She shuddered. Her stomach churned. She fled from the balcony, but the distant shouts from the harbor followed her, echoing down the spiral staircase into Antonius' bedchamber.

* * *

Constantinople was as excellent a place as any for a merchant to be. But the sight of the encamped armies and the ceaseless smacking of catapulted stone against the walls of the city persuaded Opilio that young Soroush might have been right to be so confident in the Persian military might. On the night that the Persian navy was sunk in the Bosphorus, Opilio recognized that the struggle for the city would not soon come to an end. However, he realized that the destruction of the Persian ships also presented him with the opportunity to sail out of the city unhindered.

And so, the following night, under cover of darkness, he, Thrax, and Soroush cast off and raised sails, heading east. In a few hours, they made landfall near Chalcedon and were immediately greeted by an armed Persian detachment. The commander of the detachment spoke brusquely in Persian.

Opilio looked at Soroush, who dutifully translated, "They asked who we are and what our business is here."

Opilio nodded at Soroush and turned to address the Persian commander. "We are simply a small merchant crew trying to avoid becoming a hindrance to either the Persians or the Romans."

Soroush translated again for the Persians.

Opilio did not even need to wait for Soroush's translation of the commander's response. He could see they were not convinced.

Soroush conveyed the message anyway. "They do not believe you. They say, 'At this time of night? It seems more likely you are attempting to smuggle a message to your Emperor.'"

Opilio smiled his most genuine smile and spoke with his most reassuring tone, "My lord, I assure you he is not my Emperor any more than he is your Emperor. It seems the city is soon to be in Persian hands, and we simply want safe passage. Perhaps we could offer some small token of our appreciation for your generosity?"

As he relayed Opilio's words, Soroush abruptly changed his tone and straightened. *Ardashir?* He recognized the Persian he was speaking to and decided to add to Opilio's message. He spoke again, energetically now.

"I will bring the ship into the Roman's harbor with your men aboard. "

Opilio was uncomfortable. "What are you saying?"

Ignoring Opilio completely, Soroush continued, now speaking in Greek, "But in exchange, my friend here shall keep his ship and his goods, and I am to be granted a Roman ship once the city is taken."

Ardashir scowled. "What's to stop me from killing you all right now and taking your ship under my command? And even if you captained the boat, how would we trust that you would not simply deliver my men into the hands of the Romans if they offer you the ship themselves?"

Opilio rubbed his hands together repetitively, anxious that such a negotiation was taking place without his involvement. But Soroush continued undeterred. "All of your seaworthy men lie cold at the bottom of the Bosphorus. You need me to get across. And you should trust me... because you trusted my father."

Opilio and Thrax looked at each other in confusion. Ardashir paused. He grabbed a torch from the man beside him and held it close to Soroush. He squinted and examined the young man's features—his dark eyes and hair, his sharp nose.

When Ardashir's eyes glimpsed the jackal's tooth around the man's neck, his skepticism gave way to recognition. "You are Narseh's boy."

"Yes," Soroush confirmed. "And the man who slayed my father in Tyre many years ago is across this river and behind those walls. And there is nothing that is going to stop me from taking his life."

Ardashir beheld the conviction in the young man and believed the words he spoke. "Young man, if the man who killed Narseh is indeed in that city, I will lead the men myself alongside you."

Ardashir barked his orders at his men, and a flurry of motion and activity ensued.

Opilio grabbed Soroush by the shoulders. "What the hell did you do?"

"We are borrowing the ship, but it will be returned to you. I suggest you do not hinder them. They would have taken your ship and killed you were it not for me."

Opilio looked around at the number of Persian soldiers boarding his ship and threw his hands up in frustration. "Bah!"

With military efficiency, all of Opilio's cargo was unloaded and left on the shore, with only himself and Thrax to guard it. He watched helplessly as the ship was reloaded with soldiers and their arms. Finally, Soroush and the Persian commander boarded, casting off with the merchant's beloved *corbita*, leaving Opilio and Thrax in the dark on the rocky beach to fend for themselves.

* * *

Asana could not help but notice that the gardens were not the same. The mythic sensation she felt when she first stepped foot on the marbled paths was gone. The plants and the fruit trees had suffered since the aqueduct was cut. Many had begun to wilt. There was no more babbling stream, only dry rocks where the water had once flowed. The air that was once so thick with the scent of jasmine, citrus, and iris was now tainted with the smell of fire and decay. The seven stars of the *Parvin* that shone like flawless gems were now mired in a smokey haze. This place, this sanctuary, was surrendering to the malevolence that approached from all sides.

She reached the mosaic of mother and child and was more deeply moved than ever by the image. To have not known her mother… to have not yet known a child of her own… tears formed in her eyes at these thoughts. She turned the silver ring around her finger, wondering for the thousandth time about her mother. What did her voice sound like? How did she look? How did she walk? All these questions she would never have answers for. Asana continued on until she stood in front of the pond, now dry and silent. She reminisced, thinking of how Antonius had first made love with her here. She closed her eyes. That now seemed like ages ago…

"Asana…"

Asana turned to behold Antonius standing on the path. His expression, always stoic, now betrayed an anxiety—a troubled seriousness that had never been there before. The piercing, confident gaze she had grown used to seeing in his eyes was supplanted by doubt. He held his helmet at his left hip, but he dropped it to the ground when she ran to him. She nearly jumped into his arms and clutched him as tightly as she could. She kissed him up and down his neck and face as he held her tightly.

There was a sense of urgency now, as if they must pour everything into each other because the chance might not come again. She could not hold back tears at the thought of losing what they had. Their kisses were in utter desperation. Nothing else mattered. Gone was the fear of being caught or discovered. Everything the two had ever held back, everything that they had ever imagined they might want to say to each other, must be said here. Now. Only there was no time to speak. Only time to act, to touch.

Asana pulled herself into his chest with all her might as his strong hand cradled the back of her neck, pulling her toward him. Antonius moved his other hand toward the pale cloth of the *stola* draped over her shoulder and pushed it aside. He let her go only briefly to remove his breastplate and tunic and quickly pulled her back to his bare chest. Asana felt his heart beating strongly, and she felt her own blood rushing as his hand moved down her sides to her naked thighs. His fingers found her warmth, and she felt the now-familiar weakness overtake her knees. A soft, quick moan escaped her lips between quickening, wet kisses.

In her haste to be as near to him as possible, she hopped up, wrapping her legs around his back and her arms around the back of his neck. He caught her easily, hands on her behind, his grip enclosing her form. Entwined together, they were torn between eagerness to go on and the need to prolong the moment.

Slowly he entered, and the desire escalated for them both. In tandem they moved, building together until they exhausted themselves rapturously. Antonius felt his legs about to give out and brought her to the ground, collapsing beside her. She immediately rolled onto him and kissed his neck quickly and greedily as he caught his breath. She bit at his shoulder and chest before showering him with more kisses.

Having regained his strength, he rolled over with one arm at the small of her back, pinning her underneath him. Smiling, he grasped her wrists and brought them above her head. He stared deeply into her eyes for a long time, closing them before kissing her passionately. She paused to stare up into his eyes for a moment more. The gleam in them was the same as the starlight in the sky behind them.

"Asana," he half-whispered. "There is nothing else I could want after wanting you. These gardens, this palace, this city… this world… The only place I desire to be is wherever you are."

Asana's heart pushed at her throat, and tears welled from her eyes. The world had shown her nothing but pain and uncertainty—struggle after struggle. But here, in this Roman's arms, all that pain seemed far away. She could not possibly speak through her emotions, so she pulled him close to kiss him more sincerely than ever before.

At long last, at Antonius' urging, they stood.

He took her hands in his and kissed them, saying, "When this war is over, I will make you my wife. And we will have our own garden, our own fountain, our own palace." He grabbed his tunic and breastplate from the ground, dressing as he spoke, "But for now, I must do what I must do to hold the city."

"I know," Asana said quietly.

They kissed once more. He departed, and his absence called attention to the dry streams and wilted plants of the garden. Asana looked around and sighed heavily, saying the quote to herself, *"Accept the things to which fate binds you, and love the people with whom fate brings you together, but do so with all your heart."*

*　*　*

The Persian soldiers hid below decks as Soroush guided the vessel to a pier in the harbor of Julian. The silence of the water and the harbor made the creaking planks of the ship that much louder in his ears. There were few Romans at the harbor. Most had been sent to reinforce the land walls now that the bulk of the Persian and barbarian ships had been sunk. Still, four Roman soldiers approached the lone *corbita* as it drifted into the harbor.

Soroush heard one of the Romans shout, "Show yourself!" He complied immediately. "Who are you? What is your business?"

"I am a merchant. I watched the Persian Navy sink and thought it safe now to deliver my goods," Soroush explained.

The Romans looked at one another. One of the men said to the others, "I recognize this ship and this man. I have seen them at the harbor of Theodosius."

Another turned back to Soroush and asked, "What goods do you have aboard?"

"Oil. Wheat from Egypt. Some fruits. I was told the imperial storehouses were nearly empty," Soroush said affably.

"Throw us your ropes. We will inspect your cargo before you enter the city."

"Of course." Soroush threw down the ropes, and the soldiers tied the ship to the pier. He laid out the gangway and ushered the four aboard. Two soldiers watched from the gate at the entrance to the harbor and a few more stood atop the seawalls.

Soroush showed his open palms to the Romans to demonstrate that he was unarmed. He then pointed to the hatch in the deck that led below to the cargo hold. Pulling the hatch open, there was a look of confusion on the soldier's face as he saw dozens of faces looking back up at him. A spear emerged and pierced him through the abdomen. Before the other three soldiers could react, several Persians emerged from barrels that were lashed to the mast. The Romans had no chance and were quickly slain.

The remaining Persians poured out from below deck like a river, charging full speed to the gate in the seawall. The guards could not close the gate in time, and the Persians easily entered the city. One of the men atop the walls managed to blow a ram's horn before being pierced by arrows. Isaac heard this horn from further east along the wall and could see the dangerous situation unfolding. He broke into a full sprint toward the palace, praying silently to himself that there would be enough time to repel the attack.

* * *

Isaac ran up breathlessly, shouting, "*Tourmarch* Andronicus!"

"What is it, Isaac? Breathe!"

"Persians... Persians inside the walls," he managed, breathing heavily.

"What? How? Where have they breached?" Antonius asked, pulling his sword from its sheath.

"Not a breach, sir.... They arrived on a ship... the harbor of Julian...the sea gate."

"On a ship? The Persian Navy was defeated! How many?" Antonius demanded.

"Maybe two hundred, sir. The harbor was only lightly manned. They were seen heading east. I presume they aim to take the palace, sir."

Antonius shouted to the men across the plaza. "Send for Francio. Tell him to lead as many men as he can spare from the walls to the *Augustaion,* with haste!" he ordered. At the same time, he turned to the men standing at the *Chalke* gate behind him. "Bring the *topoteretes* a fresh horse and gather any of the men who are resting or eating. The servants too! Tell them to make ready for battle."

"Yes, sir!" the guard shouted. "Gates up, half!"

The gate clattered as the chains bore the heavy bronze bars upwards. The rapid orders had set off a frenzy of motion, but Antonius froze as he thought, '*Asana*'... He sprinted under the gate, into the palace, and back towards his chambers.

⁕　⁕　⁕

Asana was leaning out of the window, listening to the commotion below, when Antonius burst into the room, the heavy wood of the door thudding loudly against the wall. "Asana!" She was startled, and he strode up to her quickly, embraced her tightly, and kissed her forcefully. "You must come with me!"

"What is happening?"

"Come. Hurry, the Persians will try to take the palace. I must bring you to the *Hagia Sophia.* You will be safer there."

She tried to collect her thoughts. "But they will see me, Antonius!"

"That doesn't matter anymore!" he barked impatiently. "We must go!"

She felt the anxiety clutch at her—an all too familiar feeling. He grasped her upper arm, and his grip pressed her copper armlet painfully into her skin. Down the familiar halls and walks, she stumbled, trying to keep up with his pace. But instead of making their way to the refuge and sanctuary of the gardens, they turned and went where she had not been before. Soon, the gates of the palace came into view. They were half

162

raised, and men hurried back and forth, shouting orders and handing out weapons and armor.

Antonius led her through the gate, and the men opened a path when they saw Antonius, some seeming perplexed at the sight of a Persian girl at his side and others too focused to notice or care. Across the open courtyard of the *Augustaion* they went. Despite her near-panic, Asana was still awe-struck by the city, even more so by the looming *Hagia Sophia* ahead of them. Antonius had only described it to her, but no description was sufficient. He led her up the few steps toward the entrance gate of the massive church.

He paused and turned to her, holding her by both arms now. "You must stay here. If we are victorious, I will come and find you, but you must not leave the church. You will be safest here. But if the city falls, they will defile everything. You must go to the harbor and try to board a boat and cross the water to the north. Do you understand?" Asana nodded. He shook her. "Do you understand? Say it!"

She said, "I understand!"

He kissed her, still holding her fast in his grip. They stared into each other's eyes, and he said calmly, "I love you, Asana." Before she could say anything, he was gone, running back towards the palace to join the other men who were scrambling to prepare.

"*I love you…*" she whispered to herself.

* * *

The Persian soldiers emerged into view on the *Mese* before the Romans were able to arrange themselves in formation. The Persians fired arrows and spears as they charged headlong toward the *Chalke* gate. As they bore down on the defenders, they unsheathed their swords. Antonius

163

roared, his sword held straight above his head. The other Roman soldiers followed suit, their combined shouts resonating off the stone walls of the buildings around the *Augustaion*. Behind the Romans, but in front of the now-closed *Chalke* gate, stood the servants of the palace, armed with knives, clubs, and anything else they grabbed in their hurry. There was a mute terror in many of the servants' eyes as they stood tense, fearfully hoping they would not be needed as the last line of defense.

Soon the shouts were punctuated by the harsh clashing of iron on iron and the heavy clap of wooden shields being struck. Moments later, there were screams of agony and the sounds of iron on flesh. The Roman infantry were highly trained, but they had little time to prepare, and the Persians were many. Men fell, bloodied, and neither side seemed to gain any advantage.

From the steps of the *Hagia Sophia*, Asana watched. Dread infused her stomach. So much depended on the next few moments, and yet again, all of it was beyond her control. She stared, trying to see if she could catch a glimpse of Antonius amongst the blurred chaos. But instead, she saw something utterly unexpected. Standing back slightly from the skirmish stood a face she would recognize anywhere, her father's.

"*Baba!*" she exclaimed in a shocked hush.

There was not even a second for her to react before she saw another face she would never forget, Antonius, with bloodied streaks across his cheeks and on his breastplate.

There was a strange deliberateness to Antonius' motions that Asana had not seen before. Each challenger who approached him was seen, met, and struck down quickly, often with a single swing of his sword. But it was not the gore or the savagery that stood out to Asana. It was the cold, methodical way that Antonius dispatched the Persian soldiers that

164

unnerved her. The killing did not seem like a desperate, necessary act of survival, but more like a tedious chore.

She watched him kill another, the impaled Persian slumping to his knees, his bearded face contorted in pain before collapsing to the ground at Antonius' feet. He looked up from his slain foe, turning his head in search of the next adversary. Asana saw him go rigid, his stillness looking out of place against the battle going on around him.

What is he looking at? she wondered, following his line of sight. *No!*

A lump formed in her throat. Standing across the square, her *Baba* had caught sight of Antonius marching up to him.

* * *

Antonius felt as though he had gone deaf. The loud clattering of steel no longer found its way into his mind. His vision had become a tunnel, and at the end of the tunnel was that damnable face… *Ardashir*. The sharp nose. The leathery skin. He was aged, yes, but his charcoal eyes still burned with vigor. Antonius could not believe his fortune. He had chased this wretch all the way through the desert to no avail. Finding and killing Narseh the torturer in Tyre was only a consolation prize. He had thought of vengeance against the *argbadh* Ardashir every single night since then. He cursed his post as *tourmarch*, which kept him in the city and prevented him from continuing his hunt through the deserts of the east.

But what luck! Now, his elusive prey had wandered right into the lion's den. Antonius wasted no time, marching toward Ardashir, his eyes fixed. As he neared, Ardashir's head tilted slightly in a gesture of uncertainty. Antonius sensed that

Ardashir could recognize him but did not recall from when or where.

So Antonius removed his helmet and stopped a dozen paces away, barking over the din of the battle, "Ardashir, the former *argbadh* of the fortress at Antioch…."

A wave of recognition and recollection washed over Ardashir's face. "You…"

"Yes, me."

Ardashir wondered out loud, "You survived…."

"I survived. And I swore that I would hunt you down. But you have done me the service of visiting me in my fortress, as I had visited yours many years ago. Your days have been numbered since I crawled out of that miserable pit, and now your time is at its end! You will follow that swine *Narseh* to hell!" A spirit of rage overtook Antonius, and he closed the gap between them, swinging his sword with tremendous force.

Ardashir scarcely had time to bring his shield forward and staggered backwards from the impact. Sword in hand, he thrust back at Antonius, who easily evaded. The soldiers skirmishing nearby paused and separated to watch the outcome of the contest between their commanders. Swing after swing came down on Ardashir's shield. All his counterstrokes were batted away by Antonius' shield with ease. Though Ardashir was a strong soldier and swordsman, he could not match the vigor of his younger opponent. Before long, the furious attacks had worn the old Persian commander down. Unable to lift his shield, he abandoned it. He grasped his sword with two hands, swaying on his feet and breathing heavily.

Seeing this, Antonius also dropped his shield, inhaling deeply before advancing with unabated fury. Two more strong swings and two struggling parries left Ardashir down on one knee, panting. The Persian made one more vain attempt to strike at Antonius' throat, and Antonius struck the sword from his hand as he did so. Disarmed, exhausted, and beaten,

166

Ardashir submitted. Resigned now to the end, he remained on one knee, closed his eyes, and muttered his final prayer to the *Ahura.*

* * *

Some memories fade just as soon as they are formed, drifting completely out of mind within a few days. Other memories are permanent, becoming more real and tangible every time they are recalled. These memories wield a tremendous power, shaping the lives of those who harbor them. And for young Soroush, there was only one memory that mattered. From where the stone *mese* met the *Augustaion,* he looked on as the Roman attacked Ardashir, eventually besting him and bringing him to his knee. As he watched Antonius raise his sword, Soroush was abducted by his memory...

He could smell the hay and feel it pricking against his skin. He was sweating, both from fear and from the warmth of the hay surrounding him. He could see out from his hiding place. The Roman was standing between the stables, sword raised over his father's neck. The haughty, imperious, nearly joyful expression on the Roman's face as he brought the sword down. The sickening noise of iron on flesh, the brilliant hues of blood on the stable floor, and the cold shock that had infused the boy became as real as if he were back in Tyre again.

He pressed the jackal tooth hanging from his neck between his thumb and forefinger as his other hand grasped the handle of the dagger he kept in his belt. In a few long strides, Soroush spanned the distance between himself and his prey. He went unnoticed. The soldiers of both armies were still staring at the fallen, now headless, body of Ardashir. Like a shadow, Soroush cast himself the last few steps, falling upon Antonius as he turned. His grip was locked onto the handle of his dagger with as much strength as he could muster. He plunged the long, narrow blade into the Roman's ribs.

A smile broke on Soroush's face, all of his teeth bared. He had succeeded in finding the point under the arm where the breastplate did not cover. It was a killing wound. He felt the warmth of the Roman's blood. It spilled over his hand, which still clutched the dagger, trying to push even the handle into his nemesis. Antonius looked surprised at this unexpected end. Soroush reveled in the moment.

He looked his victim directly in the eyes and spat with serpentine malevolence, "I am Narseh's son, and you are *nothing* now!"

Antonius put his hand to his side and brought it in front of his eyes. Dark blood dripped off his fingers. The pain gave way to recognition as his failing strength caused his legs to buckle. He staggered and fell, collapsing on his side on the hard stone of the *Augustaion,* facing the lifeless body of Ardashir. As he lay in the throes of his death, he thought the rushing thoughts that all dying men think. What needs to be done that I can no longer do? What needs to be said that I can no longer say? What was the sum of the life that now escapes me? What will come next? Who have I left behind?

"Asana…" he whispered as the last of his vision fled from his eyes…

Chapter IX
Eternal Flame
(August of 626 A.D.)

    A passing storm had announced its arrival with mild thunder, and a warm summer rain poured down upon the city. The ground was already quenched with blood, and the rainwater picked up a pink hue as it drained over the stone roads down to the sea. The vultures that had been circling high overhead now perched on the rooftops, staring patiently.

All had become quiet for Asana, even though the tumult of the battle had grown anew as Francio trampled into the square on horseback, followed by dozens of cavalrymen. The carnage resumed. The men on horseback were cutting down the now-outnumbered attackers. She stared vacantly at the scene for a moment, feeling nothing at all. Was this even real?

Asana drifted in a daze back through the atrium into the *Hagia Sophia*. She was drawn further inside by the sound of a choir chanting an elegiac hymn. There was nobody inside except the choir, who were out of sight up in the gallery, and they sang to the empty cathedral. *They are singing for the Ahura Mazda... for God...* Asana realized. The beauty of the hymn and the sincerity of the choir, their *spirit*, broke her down again. She fell to her knees in the nave of the great church and wept into her palms.

Their voices resonated throughout the cathedral and up the towering columns, joining Asana's quiet sobs on their way up to the Almighty like a prayer. The solemn tones reached the massive dome high above the nave, echoing back down to her ears. There would be no answer to her cries, no miraculous intercession, and no unringing of the bell. *We are each alone, trapped here, doomed, and God remains beyond our knowing,* she thought despairingly. *If he truly is master of all, if he truly loves us, why does he allow us to suffer so?* Asana wondered. Her sorrow boiled over into frustrated anger. *If he only knew how it felt to suffer! If he only knew the pains we mortals endured! If God were a mortal like us, would he not spare himself?*

Her sodden eyes turned upward toward the dome, as if making one last search for rescue, one last attempt to find an answer. As her gaze fell back to Earth, she noticed for the first time the golden mosaic in the apse above the altar. It depicted the mother and child, much like the mosaic in the garden. The haloed mother had a pained look of quiet resignation. The haloed child on her lap looked down upon Asana, his eyes curiously bright. His slight smile was not one of joy but rather one of peace and mercy.

This child that the Christians worshipped remained a mystery to her. The Zoroastrians in Persia worshipped the purifying fire. The riders of the steppe to the north worshipped the endless sky. The deities found along the Nile and Indus were fantastical and fearsome. But the Romans, themselves fearsome, bent their knees before the image of a child. How strange it all was...

She wandered back out through the atrium of the great church into the fading light of day. The gray and indigo storm clouds had meandered out over the sea and were set aflame with oranges and golds by the setting sun. Such magnificence formed in the sky, beautiful and moving. But on the ground, all Asana saw was the aftermath of a slaughter. Roman soldiers walked amongst the bodies, piercing with their swords all who had any life remaining amongst their enemies.

It was a grim sight, but it affected her not at all. All that such a scene could have done to her heart had already been done twice over. She was numb. Having lost everything, having nowhere to return to, and having nothing to care about, she experienced a curious sense of liberation. Nothing mattered anymore, so she walked. Away from the blood-stained *Augustaion*, north towards the waters of the Golden Horn.

Strange how she had spent so much time in the heart of the city and yet seen so little of it. The night she first kissed Antonius on the stone balcony above his quarters, she had been awed by the vastness of the city. She remembered marveling at the thought of so many people living their lives down there while she was hidden away in the palace. Now she saw it up close, and it was a marvel still.

And as she walked, she recoiled from thoughts of the past, and yet there was no future in which she could see herself, as far as she could tell. So she fixed her mind on the present. She took in everything, down to the smallest detail. The smoothness of the cobbles under her feet. The swirling of the woodgrain in the timbers of the houses. The now distant shouts from the *Augustaion* behind her. The scent and taste of salt in the air from the nearness of the water. The streets were quiet, and those who passed gave her apprehensive looks. She paid them no mind at all.

She paused to survey her surroundings when she reached the Golden Horn. The hills of the city sprawled upward to the west. The waters in front of her were a leaden color, punctuated with wisps of white stirred up by the fleeting storm. Asana watched the swirls and eddies, completely disordered and random, yet all part of the same river estuary, flowing constantly toward the sea. *We are, the whole of us, like these waters,* she thought to herself. *We rise, we fall, we are churned by the storms and winds, and we match the weather when it calms. Some crash on the rocks, and some gently roll on the sands. We live like the eddies, threaded and roiled together, and yet we all drain inexorably on toward the end.*

She looked westward at the hills within the city walls, silhouetted against the sky. One of these hills had a promontory that stood out overlooking the waters, and this seemed as good a place as any to go. She continued, step by step, until the cobbles gave way to dirt paths that felt cool under her feet. She felt her frustration in full again. Useless, fruitless anger possessed her and drew her hands into clenched fists.

How calloused the hand that weaves the threads of fate! What cruel deity would craft a life so dispiriting? To have planted such an improbable seed in a barren waste, to have it sprout and thrive in the face of insurmountable odds, to have it blossom into the most sublime and carnal flower, to have it

172

exhale a radiant love that eclipsed all else, only to have it plucked from the earth like a common weed. What accursed stars! Now the flower languished, its fruit dying on the vine, its petals wilting in her soul, and no amount of water from her eyes would nurse it back to bloom.

She marched hollowly up the steep hill with a ghostly grace in spite of the muddied fringes of her dress and her bare feet. The cacophony of the battle was a faint whisper in the eastern distance, drowned out by the wind and the patter of her footsteps. There was nothing else now. Not a desire, not a hope, not a purpose, only a path, and that path led to nowhere.

Asana reached the promontory over the waters of the Golden Horn. The waters lapped against the rocky shore below. She looked east and saw the smoldering ships still burning in the harbor and the storm clouds thundering in the distance. The storms were beyond man's control, but it was always within man's ability to deliver woe through conflict. And woe, indeed. Thousands of dead Persians and Romans were strewn carelessly. Lying lifeless throughout the city, on the battlements, and in the harbor. How many thousands of orphans were created this day? How many widows?

Asana turned to the west and watched the sun sink below the horizon. How many funeral pyres will blacken tomorrow's sunrise with their dismal smoke? How many ambitions, journeys, and hopes will burn up in the flames? Her heart sank again, crushed under a sadness too great to cure. She took a step to the edge of the promontory and glanced down at the bangle on her arm. The nightingale feathers brought her mind back to the babbling banks of the Tigris in Ctesiphon. How far away the city of her youth now seemed! And Raucah! Was there anything she loved that she had not lost? *Baba,* Bahram, Antonius…

Antonius…

She took her final breath and stepped over the edge…

* * *

Early the next morning, ships still smoldered in the waters. A little girl walked with her mother on the far bank of the Bosphorus. Now that the storm had passed and the fighting seemed to be over, life could go on. She did not quite comprehend the meaning of all the commotion, of all the stern-looking men in armor, and of all the boats that had been fighting in the days before. But she did recognize the look of deep concern that had been on her mother's face when she put her in bed in the evenings. If Mother had been afraid, something was wrong.

But today, that look of doubt was gone from her mother's face when she held out her hand and invited her down to the water. The little girl loved to go down to the water's edge and see the beautiful city across the river. Today, a haze sat on the water, and a burnt smell hung in the air. But still, the rising sun at her back illuminated Byzantium like a pearl. The view inspired awe and always gave the child reason to stare.

The full heat of the summer day would be felt soon. The girl hopped and splashed her feet in the shallow water while her mother filled the amphorae from the river. The water would be needed for the washing today and for the stalls where the family kept their horses and sheep. Something caught the little girl's eye as she was spinning and splashing. She took a few steps closer to investigate. A feather...

She reached down and picked it up, examining the beads of water that dripped off it, twisting it in her fingers. She excitedly brought it to her mother.

Her mother smiled and said, "A nightingale feather. Would you like to take it with us?"

174

The girl nodded. It was beautiful to her in a way that few other things had been in her short life. With great care, she folded her treasure inside a cloth and tucked the cloth into her waist.

Her mother extended her hand, saying, "Come. Let's go home."

THE END

The Author

Born in New York City and raised in New Jersey, J.F. Hughes graduated college with a degree in Business. He works as a property manager and moonlights as a music teacher. Creative at heart, Hughes has been actively pursuing his passion for writing and is excited to launch his debut fiction novel, *The Gardens of Byzantium.*

To learn more please visit www.JFHbooks.com or follow him on X.com: @JFHbooks

Printed in Great Britain
by Amazon

40491591R10108